"Thor, Baldacci, Flynn, Hamburg. Get ready as Banner fits right in!"

AMAZON REVIEW

"Move over Jack Reacher there's a new guy taking over."

AMAZON REVIEW

"Great stuff. Exciting and fast paced. On par with Flynn & Thor."

AMAZON REVIEW

"The writing was superior, the story line was compelling and the action was top-notch. Sorry I could only give this one a five star rating!"

AMAZON REVIEW

SWEET RAZOR CUT
A HARRY BAUER THRILLER

BLAKE BANNER

RIGHTHOUSE

ISBN-13: 978-1-63696-321-1

ISBN-10: 1-63696-321-8

Cover design by: Damonza

Printed in the United States of America

www.righthouse.com

www.instagram.com/righthousebooks

www.facebook.com/righthousebooks

twitter.com/righthousebooks

HARRY BAUER THRILLER SERIES
Dead of Night (Book 1)
Dying Breath (Book 2)
The Einstaat Brief (Book 3)
Quantum Kill (Book 4)
Immortal Hate (Book 5)
The Silent Blade (Book 6)
LA: Wild Justice (Book 7)
Breath of Hell (Book 8)
Invisible Evil (Book 9)
The Shadow of Ukupacha (Book 10)
Sweet Razor Cut (Book 11)
Blood of the Innocent (Book 12)
Blood on Balthazar (Book 13)
Simple Kill (Book 14)
Riding The Devil (Book 15)
The Unavenged (Book 16)
The Devil's Vengeance (Book 17)
Bloody Retribution (Book 18)
Rogue Kill (Book 19)
Blood for Blood (Book 20)

ONE

I OPENED MY EYES TO THE DARK, AWARE THAT somebody was there. I remained very still, breathing steadily, like I was sleeping. The dark was too dense. I shifted my eyes to the window. The drapes over the window were closed. I had left them open. The air was still, close, immobile.

I slipped from the bed and hunkered down beside it, below the window. I listened. There was only the heavy stillness of the small hours. The darkness was thick, like a physical thing. I stayed low and moved to the end of the bed. I sensed a breath but could not locate it or gauge the distance. I peered around the end of the bed. Where the bedroom door was, the darkness was less dense and I could sense rather than see that the door was open and the presence was gone.

I stood and moved quickly to the door, flattened myself against the wall, waited to a count of three, listening to the silence, hunkered down and peered out onto the landing. There was nothing there.

I moved fast to my bedside drawer, pulled it open and took out my Sig. I stepped back out onto the landing. My eyes were getting accustomed to the dark and I moved on swift, silent feet to the top of the stairs. Light from the stained-glass window on the landing touched the stairwell with ghostly light. A slight shadow moved across it. I ran down three steps at a time, no longer trying to be silent, bellowing, *"Freeze or I'll shoot!"*

I reached the second floor and in the dim half-light saw that the bedroom doors and my study were all open. One by one I checked the rooms, starting by the stairs and moving along the landing to the left. I saw nothing and heard nothing, but when I came to the last bedroom, farthest from the stairs, I heard the soft brush of fabric behind me. I dropped and swung round. A shadow, a ghost of a shadow, moved from the door and slipped silently down the stairs.

I sprang after it, bellowing, *"Stop! Stop, goddammit!"*

The figure was no more than eight feet ahead of me. In a single, fluid movement it vaulted the banisters and had suddenly gained a flight on me. I jumped down to the landing, hurled myself around to the next flight and saw the empty entrance hall touched by the dim, amber glow from the silent street outside. The front door was open and I could see the soft, yellow light of the streetlamps on the sidewalk, the black stencils of the autumn branches, the motionless, sleeping cars with their black windshields like dead eyes lost in dreams.

The presence was gone. I closed the door and checked the living room, the dining room, and the room I had set aside as a small library; and at the back of the house I checked the kitchen and the bathroom. But I found what I knew I would find: nothing.

A ninja? I smiled and shook my head. They don't make ninjas like that anymore, if they ever did. Shaolin? Unlikely. There was more legend than fact surrounding both the ninjas and the Shaolin monks, and where the ninjas had been trained assassins, the Shaolin monks were firmly rooted in Buddhist and Taoist principles, and they didn't go around killing people.

On the other hand, he hadn't killed me, where he could have if he had wanted to.

I went to my living room, leaving the lights off, and poured myself a stiff Macallan. Then I sat in my armchair beside the cold fire, looking at the street outside and thinking. The person I had just chased had skills beyond mere fighting abilities. We had not exchanged a single blow, yet I knew he could have taken me out at any time. I probably wouldn't even have known I was dead. He had a level of self-control that was well out of the ordinary, that you rarely found even in the Far East, let alone the West. That kind of control came from years of meditation, training mind and body to work together.

I could not think of anyone I knew of with that kind of training. Even my Jeet Kune Do instructor, Zamudio, didn't have that kind of training.

So questions: Who was he? And, also, what was his purpose?

Then, outside, on the far sidewalk, I saw a figure. My skin went cold and prickled. It seemed to materialize out of the shadows, an ink-black silhouette. It took a few steps, stopped when it was directly opposite me and, after a fraction of a second, turned and stared right at me, as though the eyes could penetrate the darkened glass right into my darkened living room. I felt a hot jolt in my belly, a strange mix of rage and fear. I sprang to my feet and ran to the front door. I wrenched it open and went out onto the stoop. There was nobody across the street on the far sidewalk. There were the dark, shifting shadows of the plane trees and the sleeping cars. And the silence of the small hours.

I went back inside and closed the door. I checked every inch of the house from my bedroom down to the kitchen and the gym in the basement, but found nothing of any interest. By then it was half-past five, so I went for a run, keeping my eyes peeled, watching the pre-dawn traffic, and the headlamps through the grainy haze of gray-blue light.

I ran a zigzag: west along 128th as far as Malcolm X Boulevard, then north a block, and east along 129th as far as Madison Avenue, then north a block to 130th, and so on until I came to the guys setting up the fruit and vegetable stall outside McDonald's on 132nd. When I got there I turned east and started zigzagging my way back toward James Baldwin Place. I figured the track was a couple of miles and took it easy, shadowboxing, sprinting, changing pace and weaving, and ducking and diving as I went. In a little under fifteen minutes I got home. I went down to the gym and worked out for an hour on the weight machines and the sack, showered and went up for breakfast. All the while I was allowing my unconscious mind to work on the two questions I had, distracting my chattering intellect and waiting for the answers to come. But nothing happened and I came to no brilliant realizations. There was a bland normality to the day.

Except that somebody had come to visit me between three and four in the morning. He was exceptionally skilled, could have killed me at any moment if he had wanted to, but instead he had left, taking care to let me know he was watching me.

Who was he? What was his purpose?

I ate a breakfast of strong black coffee and wholegrain rye toast in the kitchen, watching the golden morning yawn and stretch across my green lawn as the starlings began to emerge in small, hesitant clouds, silenced by the bulletproof glass of my windows. They hovered around the trees, fluttering, and were suddenly sucked back in again, like the film of their short lives had been suddenly run in reverse. Then they erupted in a huge shimmering cloud and soared, circling the blue dome of the sky in wild, synchronized abandon.

That made me smile.

I picked up the phone and called the brigadier as I sipped the last of my coffee.

"Yes," he said.

"Sir, it's Harry."

"I'm aware of that. I was just thinking about you. Synchronicity."

"Yeah? I was wondering if you had decided to put me out to pasture. You didn't like how I handled San Julian?[1]"

---

1. See *Shadow of Ukupacha*

"Not at all, Harry. Don't get sensitive on me, that's all I need. I just thought you could use a rest, and it wouldn't be a bad thing if the world saw a little bit less of you for a while."

"Was that your idea or the colonel's?"

"Fifty-fifty."

"For how long?"

"Well, oddly enough, as I say, I was thinking of you this morning. I'll come and pick you up about seven. We'll have dinner and a chat."

I nodded, though he couldn't see me. "I had a visitor last night."

He didn't miss a beat. "Do you need the cleaners?"

"No."

Now he sounded surprised. There was a short pause while he took it in. "Really? What happened?"

"I woke up at about four. I could sense someone in the room. I always sleep with the drapes and the windows open, but they were closed. I went after whoever it was down the stairs. I saw their shadow a couple of times but that was all. They were very fast and very agile. When I got down to the front door it was open and there was no sign of them, but a little later I saw them across the road, looking at the house."

"Could you make out any features?"

"No. He was a shadow. He was very silent, with extreme self-control and exceptional training."

"What about your alarm system?"

"He didn't trigger it. But it's not all that sophisticated."

"Why not, Harry? It should be."

"Yeah, I know." I looked into the bottom of my empty cup. "But then I'd be one of those guys with a cutting-edge security system."

"Like me."

"No, not like you, sir," I said and sighed. "One of those other guys."

"We'll discuss it when I see you later."

"Yes, sir."

I stood and went to the entrance hall to check the alarm. I hadn't checked it before because I knew what I was going to find. The circuits had all been fried, probably by an EMP. They were no great mystery. Given a little know-how and a decent ion lithium battery, anyone could put together a functional EMP device with a range of about six feet; enough to blow out most alarm systems. Some basic lock-picking skills and you're inside.

The brigadier was right. My home security and my alarm system were not up to par. But I was right too. I didn't want to be that guy who puts so much time and energy into protecting his life that in the end he has no life left to protect. Besides, I had always trusted a good iron deadbolt and a solid baseball bat a hundred percent more than an electronic circuit. You can't fry a deadbolt with a homemade EMP. So I took a stroll down 5th Avenue to West 125th and, somewhat reluctantly, bought four big, iron deadbolts. I didn't really need to keep anybody out, I told myself. What I really wanted was to hear them coming in.

I got home and fitted the deadbolts to the kitchen door and the front door, one at the top and one at the bottom. After that I took a drive to Zamudio's place in the Bronx. He had a house at the corner of Screvin Avenue and Barret, right by Pugsley Creek. It was a three-storey redbrick and he'd knocked his ground floor into the garage and converted it into a large gym. From age thirteen he'd travelled the world studying everything from boxing and shotokan to ITF Tae Kwon Do and Wing Chun. But after he befriended Dan Inosanto in California, and started studying Jeet Kune Do with him, he decided he had found what he called the ideal synthesis.

"Be like water, my frwend," he used to say, mimicking Lee's accent, "and honestly expwess yourself."

I had never quite grasped how beating seven bales of shit out of somebody was honestly expressing yourself, but Lee had understood it, and apparently so had Zamudio. I had not got there yet.

I pulled up in the quiet, leafy street beside the park and left the TVR in the shade of the trees. He had his garage door open and I could see him inside doing two-finger push-ups. He was in his mid-fifties, but he was still the fastest, strongest, most explosive fighter I had ever encountered.

He jumped to his feet and smiled at me.

"What happened?"

I made a question with my face and he pointed at it.

"You look worried. Something's eating you. What is it?"

I smiled and went to sit on the bench below the coat rack, but he was shaking his finger at me. "Don't sit down. Take off your leather and start warming up. You can work and talk."

"I had a visitor last night," I said as I shrugged out of my jacket.

"Did you talk to him?"

I laughed and shook my head, then started stretching my neck. "In fact, the thing that most struck me about him was his silence."

"Yeah? Silence?"

"He moved like his feet weren't touching the ground."

"That's a lot of leg muscle control."

"Yeah." I thought about it while rolling my shoulders. "He was like a Hollywood ninja. Like a shadow."

Zamudio laughed. "He really impressed you, huh?"

"Yup. He could have killed me any time he wanted to. He came into my room and closed the window and the drapes without waking me."

"So how come he didn't kill you while you were sleeping?"

"I don't know. I awoke when he was leaving the room. I can't figure what he wanted."

I bent and pressed my head against my knees. Zamudio said, "You said he was silent. So your instinct woke you up. But what I am asking you is, how come he didn't kill you? Focus on that."

I stood erect and let myself slide down into the splits.

"I've been turning it over in my head all morning. The only

thing I can come up with is that he was more interested in telling me something, letting me know he was there," I paused, lingering on the thought, "and he could return anytime he wanted to."

He snorted. "Truly powerful generals hide their strength. Weak generals make a big display. What makes him want to show you his strength? Why does he warn you in advance?"

I looked up at him and nodded. "That's exactly what I was wondering. And I can only think of one answer."

He jerked his head toward the rack of dumbbells. "Weights. You work, biceps, sixty seconds fast as you can. I'll tell you what I think."

I started hammering with twenty-two pounds in each hand while he spoke.

"Some time in the past you hurt this man, you broke him and humiliated him, or somebody he cared about. Now he wants to kill you, but first he wants you to know he is better than you, stronger, better trained, more dangerous. Killing you is not enough, he needs to humiliate you first."

I relaxed my arms. "Yeah, that makes sense."

"OK, shoulders, sixty seconds, fast as you can."

I began to lift, two lifts a second, arms outstretched to the side. Zamudio kept talking.

"So his weaknesses are first of all that he is emotionally compromised and sees only what he wants to see, and second he sees himself as more powerful than he is. In fact he is weak, and his weakness is that he needs you. He needs your admiration." I let out a noise born of pain and let my arms drop. He jerked his head at the weights machine. "OK, triceps and legs, then we spar for a while."

We worked out for another couple of hours, during which he kept telling me to think with my belly. I kept telling him that was bullshit. "You think with your brain, Zamudio. You digest with your belly."

He danced, ducked and dived. "Who is bruised and hurting?"

"Me," I said, trying to follow his movements.

He feinted with a backhand to my head and as I weaved away he kicked my feet from under me and I landed with a *whoosh!* on my back. He leaned over me and wagged a finger.

"The brain is too slow. You have to think with your belly. Your belly is the center of your universe. If you think, 'What is he going to do now? He has his right foot forward so maybe he will strike with a straight right...,' by the time you have finished thinking I have destroyed you twenty times over. You have to *feel* with your belly, and respond, without words in your head." I reached up and he pulled me to my feet. "What have you done about this intruder?"

"I bought big, iron deadbolts for the doors."

He nodded. "Good."

Bruised, stiff and with strained leg muscles I made my way back to Manhattan, trying to think with my belly.

TWO

AT SEVEN O'CLOCK THE BRIGADIER TURNED UP IN A dark Bentley Flying Spur V12. I trotted down the steps of the stoop, the chauffeur opened the door for me and I climbed in beside the brigadier. He was in a black evening suit with satin lapels and a bowtie. He eyed my business suit with an arched eyebrow and sighed softly, but he didn't say anything.

As we pulled away he asked, "Have you reviewed your security system?"

"Yup."

"A good attack is the best defense, we all know that, Harry. But the basis of a good attack is a solid defense."

"I know. Believe me, if anyone tries to get in again, I'll know all about it, and so will they."

He regarded me a moment. "You've set up tripwires attached to bottles and tin cans, haven't you?"

"No, sir." As I settled back I asked, "Is the colonel not joining us?"

He raised an eyebrow at me and we didn't talk all the way down Park Avenue until we turned into West 51st. Then he said, "Freud said that women were the Dark Continent and after a lifetime of research he had failed to understand them. I have to say I am with him. Most incomprehensible is their singular bad taste in men." He gazed at me a moment. "I don't mean to be offensive by saying that, Harry. I was married five times and never understood what any of them saw in me."

We went to Gallagher's, on West 52nd. It was one of those dim, dark wood and very white linen restaurants that the brigadier liked. I confess I like them too, and the steaks are like nothing on earth, unless you go up to Wyoming, hunt yourself a bison and cook it over an open fire. We pulled up outside the restaurant and strolled inside. The maître met the brigadier with a bow and led us to a booth.

"Your usual table, Brigadier."

"We'll have two vodka martinis while we look at the menu." We sat and to me he said, "You don't need to leave New York on this job, so you won't be able to blow anything up." He smiled. "Jane told me to make a point of telling you that."

Colonel Jane Harris was the head of operations at COBRA and frequently complained that I resorted too often to explosives to get a job done. She had not been on the scene since she was abducted by Russian Mafia and barely escaped with her life[1]. I had saved her life and, for some reason only a woman would understand, she had held that against me ever since.

"What's the job?"

"It's fairly straightforward, but it has to be done right. Marco Benini, the capo of the Benini family."

I frowned. "That's law enforcement. Why don't the Feds take care of it?"

"They came to us. They can't touch him. Quite aside from his friends in high places..."

I interrupted, "Blackmail?"

"Yes. He has dirt on just about everyone and anyone who counts in this city. But aside from that he has been very careful and whether you follow the money, the blood or the connections,

---

1. See *Breath of Hell*

they all lead to a dead end and fall well short of him. All the Feds have is rumor and circumstantial evidence, and evidence which, though it is highly probative, was illegally obtained and therefore inadmissible in court. I admire much about the USA, Harry. But that particular quirk of your legal system is asinine. Thanks to it, Benini is untouchable."

The waiter brought the two martinis while another handed us our menus. We toasted and sipped. As I put down my drink I said, "Forgive me, sir, but there must be a thousand untouchable guys like Benini in New York. What makes him special?"

He took a deep breath. "Well, partly the fact that the FBI have asked for our help, which is a gesture of goodwill on their part, and we need a good relationship with them. But partly also because of his catalogue of crimes, and the fact that he is not so much expanding, as spreading."

"What's his portfolio?"

"White slaving from Eastern Europe. That is still a problem Poland refuses to address, and the European Commission turns a blind eye. They are more worried about whether Poland is going to destroy their dream of a Federal Europe than they are about the white slave trade which operates there. He is also involved in heroin and cocaine importation from Mexico, a large percentage of which is paid for in weapons. There is the usual drug selling here at home, and the murder and torture of rival gang members, especially in the Bronx. But perhaps the most heinous of his operations is the kidnapping of young girls in Portugal, Spain and Italy, to sell them in North Africa and the Middle East as brides for whoever can afford them."

"Yeah." I looked down at my martini and extracted the olive. "I saw a bit of that in Afghanistan, and other parts. They tell you it's a cultural thing. Trouble is, criticizing that culture can carry the death penalty."

"So, if Benini were to meet with an unfortunate accident, it would save the Bureau a lot of time and money."

"I'd be happy to oblige."

I turned my attention to the menu, but the brigadier cut in. "I suggest a lobster salad to start, with a glass of the house white, and a couple of rib-eye steaks and a bottle of *Muga*. All right?" I nodded and he called over the waiter, muttering, "I don't want to get sidetracked by the food."

I sat back as the waiter took away our menus and our order. "So this guy is in New York?"

"He has a mansion on the Esplanade in Pelham Manor. He follows a very strict routine, which may make life easier for you—or not. I am not sure. Every day at eight thirty AM his chauffeur drives him, and two of his boys, to his office at 530 Park Avenue. At five thirty the car returns, picks him up and takes him home."

"His office? He doesn't run his empire from a seedy strip club like every other self-respecting mobster?"

"Oh, no!" He gave a small laugh. "He has a small, but lucrative investment company called Benini Holdings, from which he invests in companies that invest in companies that invest in companies. Sometimes they are laundering operations, sometimes they are straight criminal operations—in jurisdictions where the States can't touch them. The point is he uses the Park Avenue company to tie his operations up in a miasma of holdings, umbrellas and investments so that he, personally, is completely removed from any criminal activity which may occur. And for good measure he has his attorneys right next door, a firm, incidentally, in which he holds a fifty percent share. The firm is Shawn Shave and Shearing."

"There has to be a pun in there somewhere."

He smiled. "I've been looking but I haven't found one yet. His attorney is Colin Shearing, the senior partner."

I peered doubtfully into my drink. It was half empty, though it might have been half full. "He follows that routine every day?"

"Like clockwork. My contact at the Bureau tells me very successful crime bosses often fall into that kind of routine when they get older. That's how a lot of them end up getting shot."

I thought about it, looking across the room at a couple talking quietly, affectionately, in the corner. They weren't worried about growing careless and getting plugged.

"It gets exhausting," I said, then turned to look at him, "always being on your guard."

"It does. So he has built up his security and allowed himself to fall into a routine. Very, very occasionally he goes abroad. But most of the time he just follows his daily rhythm. His car takes him home from the office at about five thirty every day, Monday to Thursday, but on Friday he goes to *L'Artigiano* on East 64th."

"An Italian restaurant."

"Correct."

"That's more like it."

"He dines while his boys sit at another table. Sometimes somebody joins him, usually it's one of his attorneys, or a broker, and at half past nine his car takes him home."

The waiter came with the lobster salad and the wine waiter poured us two glasses of the house white. Once he was gone the brigadier said, "It should be a very straightforward job."

"You keep saying that," I said around a forkful of lobster.

"Yes, well, last time you undertook a simple, straightforward job I seem to remember you blew up half of the Andes. Shortly before that you blew up all of New Mexico and a little before that I believe you actually expanded the Black Sea by several miles."

He was smiling at his salad and sounded more proud than critical.

"OK," I said, "I'll start tomorrow by making a detailed study of the subject."

"I know you will, but the point I am trying to make, Harry, is that we are on home turf, in New York City. Different rules apply."

"I get it, sir. I will be a ghost." The words came out on their own and made me pause. He glanced at me. But I went on, like the words had meant nothing. "I imagine it will be a McMillan TAC-50 job, either at his house or somewhere along the route."

He nodded. "I would imagine. Take a few days to study it,

have a look at the route and run your plan by me before you do anything. I need to be on top of every detail, unfortunately. Not that I don't trust you, Harry. But this is New York, and I cannot pass the buck. Anything goes wrong, collateral damage, anything at all, and it's my fault."

They took the empty plates away and brought us the steaks and the *Muga*. With the wine conversation turned to Afghanistan and Iraq back in the day, when he was my commanding officer in the British SAS. We talked about surviving in the desert, men we had known like Captain Walker and the legendary Kiwi Sergeant Bradley, and eventually we came back to ghosts. I leaned back, swirling the tail end of my wine around in the glass.

"Zamudio, my Jeet Kune Do instructor, believes the ghost last night might be someone looking for revenge."

He finished his steak, wiped his mouth and dropped his napkin on the table. He signaled the waiter and said to me, "Well, that must be a pretty small pool." To the waiter he said, "Two espresso and two Macallans, no ice."

I was frowning at him. "You reckon?"

He leaned forward and spoke quietly, "Well, let's face it, Harry, they are practically all dead."

I made a doubtful face. "I hadn't thought about it like that. I guess you're right."

"Take some time tonight and think about the ones that got away, the ones who had a very high skill potential. There is also another category you haven't thought about, Harry."

"Who's that?"

"Old colleagues."

I shook my head. "No."

"Don't be sentimental. It could be SAS, SBS, SEALs or Delta, anyone you've worked with or collaborated with, and not necessarily someone with a grudge. It could be someone who has been employed to send you some kind of message, play with you or simply spook you before taking you out. Let's say a form of punishment. Either way I've posted a car on your street until this is sorted out."

I nodded. "Thanks. But if he comes again, just have them call me. I want to have a talk with this guy."

"Fine. Meanwhile, I am going to make inquiries. On the face of it, the jobs you have done which are most likely to bring reprisals are the Mohamed ben-Amini case [2] and the Heilong Li case[3]."

I grunted and nodded as I thought about what he was saying. "They were both representatives of huge organizations who do not like to be humiliated. His skills, and Mary Jones's status within United Chinese Petrochemicals, make China a prime candidate."

He made a face that said I hadn't seen the whole picture. "Yes, possibly, but don't forget that Mohamed ben-Amini was backed by two very powerful organizations, al-Qaeda *and* the CIA. And we are something of a thorn in the CIA's side. We have a couple of friends there, but the organization as a whole does not like us at all. They know we exist, but they do not know who we are, and they would very much like to be rid of us."

"OK, I hear you."

"So be on your toes, do the job and we'll take care of your ghost. When we find him, if it's at all feasible, we'll let you take him."

We had a couple more Macallans on the house and had the Bentley pick us up at eleven. In the car the brigadier called the guys who were watching the house and put the call on speakerphone.

"Sir."

"Have we had any visitors?"

"We been watchin' the house and we ain't seen a soul, sir."

"All right. We'll be making a delivery. Stay alert."

---

2. See *Dead of Night*
3. See *Dying Breath*

"You got it, sir."

Half an hour later I stood on the sidewalk and watched the Bentley pull away and turn into 5th Avenue. I climbed the steps to my front door, turned the key in the lock, went inside and closed the door. The hall was empty. The house was silent and still. I went into the living room. It was as I had left it. The kitchen was empty, quiet. I could sense nothing wrong. The ground floor was untouched and had not been visited.

I climbed the stairs with my P226 in my hand, pausing, listening as I went. All I got was that the house was empty. The second floor was clear and I climbed to the third floor where my bedroom was.

The door was open, the light was on and the drapes were closed. I had left the door closed, the lights off and the drapes open. It was blatant, a message that whoever it was could get to me whenever he wanted.

I went in, with the Sig held out in front of me. On my pillow there was a page from a newspaper. I checked the wardrobe and the en suite bathroom, but I knew already nobody was there. I holstered my pistol and went to look at the paper. The headline read: DISMEMBERED BODY FOUND BY RAIL TRACKS.

I sat on the bed and read the short article.

A DISMEMBERED, decapitated body was found in a vacant lot on Sunday, beside the railway bridge over the Major Deegan Expressway, not a hundred yards from the infamous Mescal Club. Police are working to identify the body. "It ain't easy," said Detective Harrington of the 4th Precinct, "his head and his hands have been removed, which only leaves his DNA. If he ain't in the system, were stumped."

Detectives are also checking missing persons' reports for a possible match. The victim was a middle-aged white male of approximately six feet.

. . .

The paper was dated 28th June, 2020.

I could remember exactly where I was that morning, and I could hazard a pretty good guess at who that body had belonged to. The only problem was, it didn't make any sense at all.

I stepped onto the landing and climbed the stairs to the attic door. The old, iron chub key was in the lock, where I always left it, but the door was unlocked. I opened it and climbed the last few steps.

The place had been empty. I'd had nothing to store up there. And the skylight had been closed. Now the skylight was open, and on the floor, against the far wall, there was a bedroll, and beside it an old-fashioned red alarm clock with two bells and a small brass hammer. I went and hunkered down beside it. That was when I saw the card lying beside the pillow. It was white and featureless, and when I opened it, it bore only the printed words, "Never send to know for whom the bell tolls…"

I am no lover of poetry, but I knew the poem by John Donne, and I knew what came next. I spoke the words softly.

"Each man's death diminishes me, for I am involved in mankind. Therefore, never send to know for whom the bell tolls; it tolls for thee."

THREE

Next morning at eight twenty I was parked on the Esplanade in Pelham in an anonymous mid-range Mercedes Benz, just one hundred yards from Benini's gate. At eight thirty on the nail a black Audi A8 pulled out of the drive. It had tinted windows so it was impossible to see who was inside, or precisely where they were sitting. They turned north and headed sedately toward the Boston Post Road, where they turned west as far as the interchange and there took the Hutchinson River Parkway south. I stayed a hundred yards behind them, sometimes a little more.

We cruised past Pelham Bay and the country club and crossed the Bronx on the Bruckner Expressway, to enter Manhattan via Randalls Island and the Kennedy Bridge. I closed the gap a bit along the FDR, then passed them and turned into East 61st ahead of them. At Park Avenue I turned left and stopped outside Christ Church with my hazards on. In my rearview I watched two guys in suits emerge from the Audi, one from the front passenger seat, the other from the back. They both converged on the near side door in back and shielded Benini as he climbed out. I knew he was sixty-three, but he looked older. He had a big gut, balding hair, an expensive, charcoal gray pinstripe suit and big feet. That was the snapshot my brain took of him. Next thing they were inside and gone. The Audi pulled away and disappeared south.

I found a place to park, walked back to number 530 and went inside. A brass plaque told me Benini Holdings was on the fifteenth floor. So I took the elevator up and stepped out into a marble landing that was on the beige side of gray and sported a handsome stone staircase with an Italianate balustrade. I followed a broad corridor on my right down to a blond wood door with frosted glass and gold leaf lettering that read, *Shave Shawn and Shearing, Attorneys at Law.* About twenty feet farther on was a similar door. Here the gold lettering read *Benini Holdings, Inc.*

I opened the door and looked in. There was a small reception with a blue carpet and a dark, blond wood desk behind which an attractive, dark-haired young woman sat and stared at me in surprise.

To the left of her, the reception area became a short corridor once it got past a couple of potted palms, and, when I craned my neck around the door to the right, I saw that the same thing happened there. I wondered how many offices Benini Holdings, Inc. had. I smiled at the surprised girl.

"Sorry, wrong office."

I closed the door and sauntered back to the attorneys' office. When I went in I found pretty much the same layout, only it was bigger and the girl on the reception desk looked more bored than surprised.

"I need to see an attorney," I said.

She suppressed a sigh and asked me, "What about?"

"My sister got hit by a car at a pedestrian crossing, while the lights were red for the cars."

"We don't deal with personal injury, sorry."

"How about breach of contract?"

"Not really."

"So what kind of law do you deal in?"

"We mainly just deal with private clients."

"Could I become a private client?"

She arched an eyebrow at me. "Really *rich* private clients."

"I'm pretty rich."

She smiled with her mouth, but her eyes said she wanted to castrate me with a blunt knife. "*Really* rich clients."

Then she let her eyes roam over my jacket, telling me their clients used better tailoring for their dishcloths.

"Fine," I said. "I'll go somewhere else."

"That's probably a good idea."

I left and took the elevator back down to the lobby, asking myself whether I had learned anything useful. I didn't think so, but you never did know when some apparently useless bit of information might suddenly become a lethal weapon.

Five minutes later I sat in my car drumming my fingers on the wheel and watching the steady flow of cars moving south. I remembered the brigadier the night before: "My contact at the Bureau tells me very successful crime bosses often fall into that kind of routine when they get older. That's why a lot of them end up getting shot."

But two got you twenty the smoked glass on the Audi was bulletproof, the chassis was probably reinforced steel and the floor was probably bombproof. A high-velocity sniper round would probably penetrate the glass, but because it was smoked, there was no way of knowing precisely where he would be seated. Besides which, there was no point along the trajectory where he could be taken without risking the lives of civilians. A bomb was out of the question for the same reason.

So that left the Friday visit to *L'Artigiano* on East 64th Street. I fired up the engine and rolled up Park Avenue for a couple of blocks, and came to the restaurant via East 63rd and Madison Avenue. It was in an old brownstone and I figured the owners had connections in City Hall because they had secured permission not only to have tables out on the sidewalk, but they had constructed a kind of ugly, giant wooden bus shelter on the blacktop, where their patrons could sit, sheltered from the traffic and the weather.

I parked farther down, walked back and sat in the bus shelter to have lunch. The restaurant proper was in the basement. I was pretty sure Benini would eat inside. Aside from the fact that his bodyguards would insist upon it, I figured if he was so security conscious, he would want to anyway. But making the hit inside would not only be extremely dangerous for me, it would make getting away extremely difficult, elevate the risk of getting caught by the cops and also put the other patrons at risk.

All of which made it out of the question.

I toyed for a moment with the idea of poisoning his food, but again, even if I could get the poison into his meal, there was still the risk that either one of the chefs or one of the waiters might taste the food. Or that one of the patrons might get served Benini's plate by mistake.

There was one, slim chance, the only one I could think of, and that was to park outside the restaurant early in the morning, be ready for Benini when he arrived, and shoot him and his guards as he got out of his car to enter the restaurant. I didn't like it because there was still a residual chance of bystanders getting caught in a crossfire, and it also meant the chauffeur was left alive and in a very fast, bulletproof car, to chase me down and take me out.

Not my idea of a good plan.

So how about if I booked a table inside? He would be eating alone, his boys at another table. I could feign that I knew him and get close enough to shake his hand, put my hand on his shoulder, make some kind of physical contact sufficient to deliver a lethal dose of something. If I was suitably disguised I might get kicked out on my ass, but by that time it would be too late. The dose would be delivered.

It was a possibility I would have to think about. Of the two options I had right then it was the best, but it would also take the longest to set up. I would have to get a table close to Benini's, and prepare a believable disguise. I would get only one shot, and I would have to pull it off and make it work.

At five twenty I returned to Park Avenue and watched the

Audi return. Like the brigadier had said, it was clockwork. The boys came down with him, bundled him in the back and took off. You might get a shot at that moment, but it would be more luck than skill, and getting away through Manhattan traffic at five thirty would be a miracle.

I followed them back to Pelham, for the sake of completeness, keeping a good two hundred yards behind them. I was pretty certain there was no point along the route where I could take him. The only way would be with a bomb delivered by drone, and that, aside from being extremely difficult, would almost certainly cause collateral damage.

When they arrived at his manor house, the gate rolled back and he rolled in. The gate closed behind him. I drove by and headed home, thinking.

What I was thinking was that the only way to get to him was to get close to him, and I wasn't sure that approaching him at the restaurant was going to get me close enough. I had to get close physically *and* metaphorically. I had to get inside his defensive circle.

I passed through the hardware store on the way, and when I got home I inspected the house from top to bottom and back again. I didn't find anything new, so I fitted the two new deadbolts to the attic door and stretched out on the sofa, where I closed my eyes and gave my imagination free rein on ways of intercepting Marco Benini between his home, his office, his restaurant and his home again. I even had a drone delivering toxic gas to the car. There were some pretty interesting ideas, but none that gave me that "Aha!" moment.

The problem, I decided, as I drifted off into dreams, was that my approach was exactly the opposite of my nocturnal visitor's. My approach was that the harder the target was, the more killing power I had to hurl at it, which in a city increased the risk of collateral damage a thousand fold.

My visitor slipped in unseen. His approach was, the harder the target, the more subtle the kill. To the point that he had actually moved in to my house and slept in my attic. So that was what I needed to do. I needed to move in with Marco Benini, get so close to him he would not even know I was there. Get so close he wouldn't know he was dead, until I withdrew the blade.

I woke up.

I lay for a while listening. The sun was bright outside. The willow oaks and the locust trees moved silently. I sat up, stood and went to the kitchen to make coffee. While it was brewing I called the brigadier.

"Can't be done."

"I see."

"There's collateral all the way in and all the way out. Friday nights are a possibility, but the risk is still too high."

"So?"

"I need to get inside."

"That won't be easy."

"No, it won't. I need an introduction, an identity, and I need Benini to make background checks that show I am who I say I am."

"And who will you say you are?"

I thought about it for a second. "We could use the colonel's input on this. She should stop being coy and get her ass in gear."

He didn't say anything and after a moment I realized he was waiting for an answer.

"Uh, I either have friends in South America who want to make a sale, or I have friends in Morocco who want to make a buy."

"OK, give me a day or two, we'll need to make sure your background is solid. Meantime keep a low profile and stay away from Benini. Have you seen any more of your lodger?"

"No, not so far."

"I'll be in touch."

I stared out the kitchen window, letting my coffee go cold, then left the house and went for a walk down 5th Avenue, following the traffic south, past St Andrew's. At West 125th I shoved my hands in my pockets and turned right, in among the crowds, scanning them as I went, looking for something or someone who looked different or wrong or out of place. That is not an easy thing to do in New York. It's a bit like looking for a white, wooly animal in a herd of sheep. In my mind I went over the newspaper article as I checked out each face, each cyclist, each jostling body, each passing car.

A beheaded, dismembered body found in a vacant lot, reported Sunday, 28th June, 2020. Which would have placed the killing on the Friday or the Saturday, when I started my job on the door at the Mescal Club[1]. The vacant lot was beside the railway bridge, not a hundred yards from that very club. The head and hands of the victim had been removed and by now had probably been through the marine food chain several times over. Maybe they had done it to make him hard to identify, or maybe as a warning. Or both. I wondered if his DNA had been in CODIS. He was Mexican, but with a name like Gregorio McDonald, he was presumably of Scottish descent.

I hadn't killed him, but I may as well have done. I had killed his boys and handed him over to Peter Rusanov, knowing that whatever they were going to do to him was not going to be nice. That didn't trouble my conscience. Whatever they did to him was no more than what he had done to a hundred others on his way up the ladder.

But what I was struggling to make sense of was first of all, why anyone would want to avenge his death, and second, why they would want to hold me responsible for it. The man who killed him, or had him killed, was Rusanov. I had just been a soldier, one of many Rusanov had employed, and in the end I had taken down Rusanov too.

It didn't make sense.

But one thing was clear. This was personal. It was very personal. He had come into my house. He had not just broken in,

---

1. See *Dead of Night*

done his business and left. He had taken up residence in my attic, and he had come down to warn me—to lure me to a warning—that McDonald's death was my death; that bell was tolling for me.

Or was it more than just McDonald? Was I being judged and sentenced for more than one death? Was there another COBRA judging COBRA? I went over Donne's words again.

"Each man's death diminishes me," he'd written. "For I am involved in mankind. Therefore, never send to know for whom the bell tolls; it tolls for thee."

I had reached the subway on the corner of Lenox, and was strolling south, thinking about making for Marcus Garvey Park. I had spotted a guy leaning against the optician's, watching the subway mouth. He had a woolen hat on his head and a loose jacket. There was something predatory about his motionless posture and his fixed attention, and that made me aware of him. He didn't seem to be aware of me, so I moved on. But by the time I had reached the bank I heard the scream. I turned and the guy with the woolen hat had a woman by the hair and was punching her hard. I broke into a run and saw that he now had a knife. She was screaming hysterically, bent over and trying to pull away, but he had a firm grip on her hair and he wasn't letting go. He was closing in for the kill.

I bellowed at him to stop, saw him look up and his eyes locked on mine. He let go, turned and ran. He was fast and in a couple of seconds he slipped into the crowds on 125th. I hesitated, thinking about going after him, but looked back and saw the girl on her knees, holding her head and crying. There was a small crowd watching her, but nobody was helping, so I went back and hunkered down beside her. Her lip was cut and swollen. Her left eye was swollen too, and bruised.

"You OK?" She looked at me like I was speaking Chinese. I said, "Do you want me to call the cops, a friend or family?"

She blinked, shook her head and touched her lip. "No, thanks. I'm OK."

"Well at least let me get you to a doctor. There's a clinic two blocks from here."

"No." She shook her head and got unsteadily to her feet. "I'll be OK. I just need to go home and clean up a bit. There's nothing broken."

I picked up her purse and stood. I handed it to her and she took it. She was breathing hard and was having trouble staying steady. I shook my head. "You have concussion. You should see a medic."

"Please don't insist. You are kind to worry, but I just need to sit quietly for a bit and I'll be OK."

There was a hint of an accent. I gave her a reluctant smile. "There aren't a whole lot of places to sit on a New York sidewalk." I pointed toward 124th. "There's a restaurant with a terrace just here. Let me help you there and let's see how you are."

She hesitated, then nodded. "Thanks. Are you a doctor or something? Most people don't give a damn."

I didn't answer. I let her lean on me and we made our way carefully to the Caribbean Fisherman. They had tables out on the sidewalk and a couple of parasols. We sat and I called the waiter.

While he took his time coming I looked at her. She had unusually black hair, like an American Indian. I guessed that when she wasn't bruised and swollen her face was probably nice to look at. She was small, with slim arms and legs and a nice figure.

"What's your name?"

"Angel," she said, and held out her hand.

"Harry," I said, and we shook.

FOUR

She ordered a coffee and I persuaded her to have a shot of scotch. It made her cough and splutter, but after a second sip it seemed to settle her.

"I don't normally drink," she said, and some color came into her cheeks.

"Who was that guy?"

"I don't know, some mugger."

I smiled and shook my head. "I don't want to pry, but that guy was waiting for you, and unless you're wearing a very expensive wig, he wasn't trying to steal anything from you." I paused, watching her face. "He had a knife."

The color that had been put there a few moments earlier by the whiskey, drained away again. She looked down at the table and licked her lips. I waited but she didn't say anything.

"It's none of my business. You don't need to tell me. But New York is a dangerous place. People get into trouble, they don't ask for help..." I trailed off and shrugged.

She took another sip of whiskey and shuddered.

I said, "You're not from New York, are you?"

"No."

"You haven't been here long."

She gave a small laugh that was on the helpless side of unamused. "No."

"OK, Angel, I won't press you. But will you please allow me to give you some advice? New York is full of predators. You are safer in a tropical rainforest than you are in New York. I am not kidding, I have lived in both."

She laughed and I smiled, and repeated, "It's true, I am actually not joking. Hazarding a guess, I figure that guy offered you help of some sort, or his boss did, and now he wants you to pay him back. Only nobody told you about the thousand percent interest."

She sighed and sagged back in her chair. I said, "You should talk to the cops."

"He told me if I went to the cops he'd know and he'd…" She shuddered.

"You have no family and no friends here?"

"No. Not here, not anywhere." She looked up at me and there was something guarded in her eyes. "He asked me the same questions."

"Of course he did. Was it him or his boss?"

"His boss, Johnny." She gave me that look again. "How do I know you're not…" Her face clenched up and she closed her eyes. "I'm sorry. That sounds so rude and ungrateful after you've helped me."

"Not to me. To me it sounds like you're growing smart. The answer is, you don't know. And if I ever ask you for anything, think real hard before saying yes."

She studied my face for a long moment. "Are you from another planet?"

"I never thought about it till now, but my dad was small and green, with kind of wiggly things on his head…"

She laughed, then winced and touched her face and her eye. After a moment she became serious again. "Are you really a good guy?"

I nodded. "Yeah. I do my best. So, Angel, I'm going to take

you to see my doctor now. He's down on 5th Avenue and 106th. I will wait outside and anything you discuss with him will be totally private and privileged." She drew breath to protest but I cut her short. "What's in it for me? I get to sleep tonight without worrying about whether you have a cracked skull. If you like I can call him and tell him to expect you, and you take a cab."

"Harry, I can't afford to see a private doctor."

"I already paid him. He's on a retainer. I'm a hypochondriac."

She closed her eyes and smiled and sighed. "OK, thank you. I will pay you back. And if you want to come along I guess I'd be grateful of the company. Though I still don't understand why you're doing this."

I shrugged. "I always figured it's what normal people do. Only most people aren't normal. So, tell me something, in the strictest confidence between you and me: who is this Johnny and where can he be found?"

"No!"

I raised both hands. "I am not going to go and see him or tell the cops. I just like to be informed."

"You're a cop!"

"Not exactly."

"You're FBI?"

I made a show of sighing and thinking. "I'm a kind of consultant. The work I do does not have immediate effects, like the cops racing off to arrest someone. But by gathering information about men like this Johnny, we start to put together a picture, and when we have all the pieces we can close down large networks of drug dealers, pedophiles, extortionists..."

"Oh my god..."

"So when he goes down, and it won't be for a while yet, the last person he's going to be thinking about is you."

She thought about it while I called my doctor and made an appointment for half an hour later. When I hung up she told me, "His name is Johnny Martinez, I met him at his café, 1st Avenue and 115th. It's called Johnny's Bar. He lives upstairs. He was always trying to get me to go up there, but I never did. I had a small apartment, a couple of rooms, on East 117th, and I guess Johnny's was a cheap place to eat, and he was always funny and friendly. He gave me the creeps, really, but I was alone and..." She shrugged, like she was apologizing. "He made me feel welcome, sometimes he'd give me a coffee or a cake on the house."

"So what went wrong?"

"I'm unemployed. I was doing whatever jobs I could pick up here or there, so I was always short of money. It was approaching the end of the month. I knew I was going to have to pay the rent, and I didn't think I was going to have enough to cover it. So I hadn't gone to Johnny's for a week or more, trying to save money." She gave her head a small shake. "I just happened to bump into him on the street. He asked me where I'd been. I just felt so desperate and alone, I started crying and told him I had no money." She shrugged. "He lent me a few hundred to cover the rent and get something to eat, and told me there was no hurry to pay it back. But pretty soon he started pressuring me, and when I told him I couldn't pay it all at once, I'd pay him twenty dollars a week, or a month, he turned nasty and said either I paid him in kind, or he'd send his boys to settle the debt."

I nodded. "Nice guy."

"It was stupid of me to accept money from him. I knew what he was like. I'd seen what he called his special customers." She sighed again, like she was despairing at her own stupidity. "The ones who wanted cocaine came into the bar. They always had a drink and were noisy, and would have some kind of takeout, and that was where he put the coke. He told me that. The ones who wanted heroin went to the side door on East 115th. He didn't let them in the bar. They went upstairs and one of his boys would give them a small plastic bag. They were like skeletons. They looked anorexic. They were so weak and frail, but a couple of times I heard Johnny send a couple of his boys to beat one of them up, because they couldn't pay him what they owed him. Trouble is, when you're desperate, you don't always think."

"That's why they call it being desperate. OK, let's get a cab and I'll take you to see the doc."

I delivered her to Doc Brown's waiting room, told the receptionist to take care of her, let me know when they were through, and I would come and collect her. Then I went downstairs and took a cab back to my house on 128th, where I picked up my TVR Griffith and growled my way to First Avenue, to Johnny's Bar.

The funny thing about high-crime neighborhoods is, if you go there in a thirty, forty or fifty-thousand dollar car, by the time you get back to your car from wherever it is you've been, it will either be gone, vandalized or both. But if you show up in a hundred-thousand dollar car they won't touch it, because they assume that if they do, next day somebody's going to come knocking on the door with a pair of pliers in his back pocket, and a greeting from *El Jefe*.

I parked outside the bar and walked inside. There were a couple of guys at a table in the corner smoking, drinking beer and playing cards. One of them was the boy with the wooly hat who'd pulled a knife on Angel.

I saw him freeze but ignored him and went to the bar, where there was a fat guy in his fifties with greasy hair and a face full of grizzle he should have shaved three days earlier. He was leaning on the counter with both hands and watching me with his mouth sagging open. He made it look both insolent and stupid at the same time.

"You Johnny?"

"Who's askin'?'

"His great-uncle died and left him a sheep farm in Australia. Are you Johnny?"

He grinned like he'd suddenly realized he was really smart. "I ain't got no great-uncle in Australia."

I frowned like that didn't make sense, leaned forward and smashed my right fist into his face. His nose exploded in blood and gore and he staggered back cupping his face in his hands and saying, "Oh, Jesus!"

The two boys were on their feet, scattering chairs and cards and running at me. I took a couple of steps to my right to put Wooly Hat behind his pal. His pal had the kind of embarrassing moustache some kids get when their hormones start going crazy. He was about sixteen and had a skull tattooed on his fist.

I exploded into him as he reached out with both hands to grab me and smashed a straight right into his jaw. He sagged back and fell to the floor. Wooly Hat sidestepped him, reaching into his pocket for his blade. I smashed a right front kick into the side of his knee and heard it crack. He let out a high-pitched scream and reached down to his leg, like he wanted to hold it together. I dragged him, hopping, by the seat of his pants and the scruff of his neck, to the bar. There I pulled my Fairbairn and Sykes from my boot and drove it through the back of his hand and into the wooden bar. There I levered it right and left, severing the tendons. He screamed again. I pulled the knife free. He passed out and fell to the floor. Then I vaulted the bar.

Fat Johnny backed away from me shaking his head, saying, "No, no..."

"Yes, Johnny. We need to talk."

"Who are you? I can pay. Who sent you? Just tell me."

I showed him the blade. "Close the bar. Upstairs."

I vaulted the bar as he lifted the flap. I put the knife away and pulled the Sig Sauer P226 from under my arm. He locked the doors and flipped the sign on the door to closed. Then he stood staring at me and shaking.

I said, "You can live or you can die. Make a choice."

His voice was a rasp. "I want to live."

"Then you take me upstairs and you give me your stash of money."

He started shaking his head and licking his lips. "No, I ain't..."

"Give a little trouble." He stopped dead, not understanding what I was saying. I went on, "Give me just a little bit of trouble, and I will take you behind the bar and amputate every part of you that lends itself to amputation. Are you hearing me, Johnny?"

He was shaking too hard to answer, but he made a strange "Yeyeye…" sound and nodded.

He led the way up a dingy staircase with a threadbare carpet over wooden stairs, and opened a door that had needed painting back when people had radiograms. He fumbled in his pants for his keys, dropped them, picked them up, fumbled some more and got one in the lock, then turned and pushed into a small, carpeted hall. There was a kitchen straight ahead, and next to it a small john. There was a bedroom on the right that was dark and smelt like unwashed sheets, stale sweat and last night's marijuana. On the left there was a living room with a big TV, a big vinyl easy chair and a small table designed for TV dinners. He pointed tentatively at the bedroom and said, "It's in there."

"Let's go get it."

I followed him into the bedroom. He switched on the light. The drapes were closed and the air was stale and sour. The sheets looked the way they smelt. They were stained with sweat and there were soiled clothes on the floor. He stood in front of the wardrobe and swallowed.

"I…" He looked at me. "I gotta make a buy in a couple a'days. If I don't make the buy they get mad. They think you're cheating them."

I leaned on the jamb. "What's your point?"

"They'll kill me, man! If you take my money, I can't make the buy. They'll kill me."

"And what do you think I'm going to do if you don't give me the money?"

"All I'm asking is you leave me enough to make the buy, man. It's all I'm askin'."

"Do you know who Angel is?"

"Eh…?"

"Angel, pretty, small, black hair. She used to come in here to get food."

His face creased into an ugly, desperate grin. "Angel! Sure. Just a few days ago I helped her out. Cute kid, I'm like an uncle to her!"

I took a couple of steps so I was standing real close. "Your boy hurt her. He busted her lip, punched her in the eye. He pulled a knife on her."

There was panic in his eyes that said he was in territory he did not understand. He gave his head a small shake and said something like, "B-b-b..."

"To tell you the truth, Johnny, I am having trouble thinking of a single reason I should leave you alive. So if I were you, I would stop wasting time and I would give me that money now, before I lose interest."

He wrenched open the wardrobe, pulled away a loose panel from the back and dragged out a sports bag. He unzipped it and showed me inside. It was full of cash counted into neat packs and bound with elastic bands.

"There's five hundred grand in there. Tell her I'm sorry. I'm really sorry about Lou. He wasn't meant to do that. I didn't know. I was only trying..."

"Did you ever kill anyone, Johnny?"

"What? Uh—" He shrugged. "No. I mean, couple of junkies. They stop paying, y'know. You gotta get tough. But junkies die easy. You hit them too hard, whatever."

I smiled. "They do, don't they? Backhander and boom, they're gone." I laughed. He laughed too, relieved at the release of tension, a glimmer of hope in his eyes.

He said, "Right? A slap and they drop dead!"

I chuckled. "Tell me the truth, what was the youngest kid you ever sold H to?"

"Oh, man, in this neighborhood? There's kids out there, ten and eleven. One kid come to me, knocked on my back door, he must'a been no more'n ten years old. Tells me his mom is going cold turkey but she's got no money. I told him no money no dope. So he reaches in his pocket and pulls out twenty bucks, buys a fix and asks me if he can shoot up in my can. I says, 'What about your mom?' He says, 'Screw her. I need a fix, man!'"

"So you let him use your can?"

"Sure. His mother was gonna die, but I still had a couple of years outta this kid, right? H is cheap these days, but twenty bucks a shot over two years, it adds up."

He'd relaxed, feeling the conversation meant he was in the clear. I held his eye until it became uncomfortable and I let him read what mine were telling him. His face collapsed and he began to sob. I drove both fists into his floating ribs and ruptured his liver. When he went down I slipped the Fairbairn and Sykes down behind his left collarbone. He quivered and shuddered for a moment, and then he was gone. One less.

I carried the bag out to the TVR, slung it in the trunk and drove down to 5th Avenue, to collect Angel.

FIVE

She stopped on the sidewalk and stared at the TVR. She gave a small, incredulous laugh.

"This is your car?"

"Get in, I'll drive you home. I have some things I need to explain to you."

"So you're rich."

"I'm not in the one percent, but I'm doing OK. Are you going to get in?"

She stared at me a moment, then back at the car. She was looking better. She had more color in her cheeks. Whatever the doctor had done, the swelling had gone down and the purple bruise had been concealed under some kind of cream. She stepped forward and there was an awkwardness about her movements, like she had never climbed in a car before. She slipped into the white leather seat beside me, with her hands on her lap and said, "Wow..."

I smiled and pulled away from the curb. "Where are we going?"

"Oh, uh... I have an apartment on West 126th, it's a small attic, just one room really."

"No kidding! We're almost neighbors."

It didn't seem to register and she went on. "I had to move away from Johnny, but this was all I could afford. I don't think the landlady will let you come up."

"That's OK, I'll leave you at the front door. There are a couple of things I need to explain."

She frowned at me. It was that, "Oh hell, now everything is going to go sour," look. "What do you need to explain?"

"I went to have a talk with Johnny." She didn't say anything. She just stared at me. "I explained to him that what he had done was unacceptable, and could have serious consequences in the law."

I glanced at her and she gave a small giggle. "You said that?"

I shrugged. "Words to that effect. So we had a short discussion and the upshot was that, to avoid things going any further, he offered to make a donation."

She screwed up her brow. "A *donation?*"

"Yup, a fund to help young women who have settled in New York and have no family to rely on. The idea is that it avoids them falling into debt, or worse."

"Wow, you convinced him to do *that?* I can't believe it."

"I can be very persuasive when I have to be. So it will take a couple of days to set up, but it should be worth about twenty grand to you every year. It should cover your rent, at least."

She was silent until we pulled up outside her apartment. It was set in the middle of a row of brownstones, but somebody had ripped out the door and the windows and replaced them with white, plastic frames and glass. I looked at it and reflected that there are many kinds of crime, and most of them go unpunished.

I reached in my breast pocket and pulled out an envelope with three grand in it.

"He gave me this for you. It's something to compensate you for the nasty experience and tide you over till the fund kicks in."

She took it and stared inside. Then she narrowed her eyes at me. "And there are no strings attached?"

"None."

"I mean with either of you. I hate to sound ungrateful, but I just don't get it. Why are you doing this?"

I thought about it and wondered the same thing. After a moment I shrugged.

"Maybe I'm doing it for a little girl I once wasn't able to help, a few years back, and her eyes still haunt me today. Or maybe cities like New York are not the standard by which humanity should be judged. Maybe the normal thing is for people to help each other, and in abnormal ratholes like LA, New York, London, people become spiritually stunted and deformed."

"Do you really believe that?"

I gave my head a single shake and shrugged. "I don't know. I'd like it to be true. I'm no saint, Angel, but I don't like seeing people get victimized. And if I'm in a position to do something about it, I will."

She hesitated. I smiled to show I was joking and said, "If it makes you feel any better I can take you out to dinner and make a pass at you. Only to restore your lack of faith in humanity, you understand." She smiled uncertainly and I gave her my card. "If you need anything, call me. By the way, what's your surname? For the fund."

She hesitated a moment, then said, "Lee."

"L-E-E?"

"Yeah."

I saw her in my rearview mirror, standing at the top of her stoop, watching me drive away. As I drove the two blocks back to 128th, I asked myself several times what the hell I thought I was doing. All I could answer myself was that I didn't know, but it felt like the right thing to do.

On the way I made a call to the brokers I'd had to employ, on the brigadier's advice, to take care of what he called my spoils of war, which by now amounted to a fair bit and took some pretty creative accounting to deal with—mostly in places like Belize and the Bahamas. I told them what I wanted done and they told me they'd see to it.

At seven fifteen that evening the brigadier telephoned.

"I'll be calling for you in fifteen minutes."

"I haven't done my hair."

"Don't wait outside. The chauffeur will come to the door."

I had time to pull on my jacket and run my fingers through my hair and there was a ring at the bell followed by a brief knock on the door. I looked out the bow window, saw the Bentley and the uniformed chauffeur on the stoop, and opened the door. He didn't look at me. He looked up and down the street, obviously saw some signal I did not, and led me down the steps to the back door of the Bentley. He opened it and I climbed into the bullet-proof, bombproof security of the best car on Earth. The brigadier was sitting back in the corner frowning at me. I sat, the door thudded closed and he asked me, "Who's the girl?"

I scowled. "You're spying on me?"

"Yes. Of course. Who is she, Harry?"

I sagged back into my own corner and sighed. "A victim."

"Of?"

"A mugging. A guy pulled a knife on her, beat her up."

"So you decided you'd go and kill him."

I hesitated. "No."

"Explain. We do not condone murder, Harry, even of scum like John Martinez."

"She was in trouble. She has no family. He forced money on her she hadn't asked for and then started coming on strong, demanding repayment in kind. She rejected him and he sent the boy after her. I was there when the boy found her. I bought her a coffee and a shot and she told me the story. So I went to have a talk with Johnny."

"And?"

"And things got out of hand. The boy and his pal came at me with a knife. Johnny admitted, without losing any digits, that he trafficked drugs and had killed a couple of junkies when they couldn't pay. I told him to give me his stash of money."

I drew breath, but I couldn't bring myself to lie to the

brigadier. On the other hand, I knew that if I told him I'd killed the rat in cold blood, my career with COBRA would be over. I looked him in the eye, but he spoke before I could.

"The morality of our organization is dubious at best, Harry. We are employed by a small group of nations to eliminate the worst that humanity breeds. That's why we have criteria which must be met. They must have committed crimes against humanity."

I interrupted him. "Is that a quantitative thing, sir? Is killing five hundred people five hundred times worse than killing one? Is tying a person to a table and branding them with hot irons worse than getting a ten year-old kid hooked on heroin and watching them slowly lose their soul and die, while taking their pathetic payments of twenty bucks a fix? Is it worse to rape a woman in a prison than to exploit her naivety, get her into debt and rape her in your squalid bedroom?" It was his turn to sigh, but I plowed right on. "Because if that man, John Martinez, had had a uniform and was called General Juan Martinez, he could well have been on our list."

He was quiet for a moment. "Don't lecture me, Harry. I agree with you, completely. Frankly I think the world is a marginally better place with John Martinez out of it. My concern is not John Martinez. My concern is COBRA, and within COBRA, you."

I went to make some bitter remark about how he needn't worry about me but he raised a hand.

"Stop. Lay your pride aside for a moment and listen to me. You think you've been around the block a few times and have learned a thing or two. Believe me, I have lapped you more times than you've had hot dinners, and I still have plenty to teach you. So shut up and listen."

I shut up and listened.

"What happens if our agents start choosing their own targets, Harry? No, you can take that 'heard it all before' look off your face and start thinking a little beyond your comfort zone. Let me make it easier for you. What happens if all our agents toe the line, and I turn a blind eye when you start picking your own targets because we all agree you are somehow special?"

That sobered me. It embarrassed me and I couldn't answer, but he insisted.

"Think it through, Harry. With no check on you, with no limitations, however artificial they may be, where would you stop? And even assuming you didn't start killing the slob who beat his four year-old daughter in the park, assuming you only killed drug dealers and murderers, how long do you think it would be before a young Fed with an IQ of a hundred and fifty-five nailed you? You think that's impossible, with the resources they have."

"No."

"And once they had you, how long before the people who are supporting us now in the Five Eyes dropped us like a hot brick? Within a week, we would have the Bureau swarming all over us and you, Jane and I, not to mention all our agents, would spend the rest of our lives in prison without hope of parole."

I nodded. "I'm sorry, it was a stupid thing to do."

He shook his head. "I don't know what you're talking about. As far as I am aware we were talking in the abstract. As I understand it, you were playing Galahad again and that man attacked you with a knife. Fortunately the police have decided not to prosecute. But if it ever happens again, I will shop you myself." I looked at him and he held my eye. "Because if anyone puts COBRA at risk, Harry, I will fucking gut them and feed them to the vultures. Do we understand each other?"

"Yes, sir."

"Good. Ah, I think we're here."

We pulled up outside an old, double-fronted brownstone at number forty-four, on West 76th Street. We climbed out and the brigadier climbed the ten steps of the stoop at a gentle run, while I followed. He rang the brass bell and after a moment the heavy oak door was opened and we were admitted by a man in a white jacket to an elegant hall with an amber marble floor strewn with Persian rugs. The man in the white coat took the brigadier's coat and hung it on a coat stand with a mirror, then led us through a door on the left into a study that was all oxblood leather and dark wood, overlaid with the sweet smell of pipe tobacco. If this was the brigadier's New York residence, it didn't surprise me at all. It had the brigadier's style all over it. What came as a surprise was the colonel sitting in one of those armchairs.

She stood as we came in. The brigadier said, "Ah, Jane, you're here. Good," and made his way toward her, gesturing absently to a chair as he went. "Harry, sit," he said, taking her hands and giving her a light peck on the cheek.

She muttered, "Brigadier," and then, "Harry," and sat back down. She was in a dark blue suit and I couldn't help noticing her legs looked as good as ever.

I nodded to her. "Colonel, it's good to see you again."

She didn't answer. I sat as the door opened and the man with the white coat came in carrying a tray of decanters. He set it on the sideboard and retired. There was an awkward silence while the brigadier mixed the drinks and the colonel and I avoided looking at each other. He handed her a tall gin and tonic, gave me a generous Macallan and helped himself to a dry martini. Then he sat, crossed his legs and cleared his throat.

"The colonel and I have discussed the Benini case and we agree with you, any hit attempted on his daily route would present an unacceptable risk of collateral damage. We had hoped you would come up with some ingenious angle we had over-looked. I'm sure if it had been there you would have found it. If you could've you would've, but you couldn't so you didn't." He smiled comfortably, like he was pleased with himself, and went on. "So, as you say, you will have to go inside, undercover."

He sipped and looked at the colonel.

"We have a contact in Afghanistan, Fateh Shir. He has been in the pay of the CIA for over ten years. He supplies Araminta Browne—you remember Araminta?"

"How could I forget?"[1]

"Quite. Well, he supplies her with intelligence and he supplies...," she hesitated, "...operators within the CIA with crude opium. So you will be representing this man. You will go and visit Benini's attorney, ask for a private interview, give him Fateh's name and make an initial, vague proposal. The attorney will be cautious, obviously. He'll want to get back to you. So you leave him a contact number for a phone we will give you. He will make inquiries and discover that you are in fact Fateh Shir's highly trusted representative. Once he has established that he will invite you to a meeting with Benini. You will make him an offer of slightly more than one metric ton of crude opium, delivered over a period of one year, to be paid for in twelve installments of four million dollars. The estimated street value of this shipment is well in excess of twelve hundred million dollars, particularly with the Taliban shutting down the opium farms. You will play hardball and ask for payment for the first shipment in advance."

I nodded. "I want four million upfront. That's a lot of money so he'll want to negotiate. So we get to have meetings."

She nodded. "Correct. At first he will refuse. You haggle and go back and forth to your principal trying to negotiate a deal that satisfies everybody and allows you to make the sale. In doing that you have the chance to build some trust, maybe shake up his routine or at least get close enough to..." She trailed off.

I sipped my scotch and thought. "OK, so if he makes a background check he finds that Fateh Shir is legit. So what if he calls Fateh Shir and suggests dealing direct?"

"In the first place it is almost impossible to contact Shir directly. If Benini tried he would be put through to an operative at COBRA posing as Shir. He would tell him that this was a breach of trust and he is very upset, and please to deal with his agent."

I turned to the brigadier. "All right, so far so good, but this

---

1. See *The Silent Blade*

isn't going to change much. I am going to be closer to him, but he is going to be surrounded by his praetorian guard all the while." I paused and turned back to the colonel. "I can't take him out without taking them out too."

It was the brigadier who answered. "That is understood, but what it does avoid is collateral civilian damage, and risk to the general public."

I stared at him, and then at the colonel. I was expendable; the general public was not. They were collateral damage and collateral damage was not good. I was a calculated, acceptable loss. I nodded. "OK."

She handed me the usual manila envelope.

"Everything you need is in there," she said. "Any doubts, call the brigadier."

I gave a small sigh. "That is understood."

We talked strategy for another hour or so, and then I left.

SIX

Next morning I put on a business suit, grabbed a black attaché case, climbed into the TVR and rumbled down Park Avenue with the soft top down, enjoying the early fall sun. I parked outside 530 and found my way back to Benini Holdings once again. In the lobby I noticed this time that his attorneys had no brass plaque. They really didn't want people dropping in off the street.

I rode the elevator to the fifth floor, emerged onto the marble landing and made my way to the offices of Shave Shawn and Shearing, Attorneys at Law. I opened the door and walked into the blue-carpeted reception. The same bored girl was sitting behind the blond wood reception desk. Her face hardened and her right eyebrow arched when she saw me.

"Can I help you?"

"I need to see Mr. Shearing. It is an urgent matter concerning Mr. Marco Benini."

"Sir, I thought I had made it clear…"

"You did. You made it very clear. Now I need to see Mr. Shearing about a matter of extreme importance—extreme importance to Mr. Benini—and believe me, sweetheart, give me the runaround and your job is on the line."

I smiled without feeling and she picked up the phone. Her eyes were mad and never left me.

"Stella, I have a...*gentleman* here who says he needs to see Mr. Shearing urgently on a matter concerning Mr. Benini... Yes, *our* Mr. Benini, Marcus Benini."

She sat staring at me for a good thirty seconds, holding the phone to her ear. There was a murmur on the line and she said, "Can you give me some idea of what it's—"

I didn't let her finish. "No."

"Some idea would—"

"No. It is extremely confidential, and I really don't have time for this. I have to see Mr. Shearing *now*. If I leave this office without seeing him, believe me, you will regret it."

Her cheeks colored. "Is that a threat, sir?"

I leaned forward over the counter. "Yes, sweetheart, it's a threat. It is also a fact."

She blanched a little. Into the phone she said, "He is very insistent, Stella. Tell Mr. Shearing he says it is very urgent and concerns Mr. Benini."

After a moment she hung up. Another thirty seconds passed while we stared at each other. Eventually down the hall a door opened. A shapely woman in a well-cut blue suit and a frilly white blouse stepped out and walked toward me. She had dark hair and a string of pearls around her neck. She said, "Mr...?"

"Smith," I said, and smiled blandly. "You must be Stella."

"I am Mr. Shearing's personal assistant. What do you want to see Mr. Shearing about?"

I blinked at her three times, retaining my bland smile.

"Stella, I am going to be very honest with you. What I want to see Mr. Shearing about is none of your damned business." I showed her the attaché case. "What I have in here concerns Mr. Benini and his attorney. It does not concern anyone else. And you had better get the idea into your pretty head, that if I walk away—in the next thirty seconds—and these documents do not reach

Mr. Benini, your cute little ass is going to be on the line along with hers."

Her eyes were bright and her cheeks were pink.

"Mr. Smith!"

"You have about ten seconds, sister. I have told you several times that this concerns Mr. Benini and that it is urgent."

"Please follow me."

I smiled at the receptionist. "Thanks for your help."

I followed Stella down the short passage and through a blond wood door into an antechamber with prints of paintings by Monet on the walls. There was a desk with a computer and a brown leather sofa opposite. Beside the desk was a door.

"Please wait!"

She tapped on the door and went inside. A moment later she came out again and said, "Mr. Shearing will see you now."

I couldn't think of anything smart to say, so I ignored her and went inside.

It was everything you'd expect a successful attorney's office on Park Lane to be. There was lots of mahogany and oak, lots of leather-bound books, original paintings on the walls and a seventeenth-century desk before the window. Behind the desk was a small, bald man with big ears and crooked teeth. He did not look happy, but his self-righteous anger was a thin veneer over his curiosity and his anxiety.

"Mr. Smith," he said as he stood, "I understand you have been threatening my staff. I hope you have a good explanation for your behavior."

I ignored him, pulled out the chair opposite him at the desk and sat, forcing him to sit with me. "Well," he said as he did so. "Kindly explain yourself."

I carefully placed the attaché case on the floor, crossed my legs and narrowed my eyes at him. "Shut up, Mr. Shearing. Do you know who Fateh Shir is?"

He sat forward, eyes wide open. "*What?*"

"Fateh Shir, Mr. Shearing. Don't make me repeat it. Do you know who he is?"

"*Should* I?"

"Yes, you should. He has a business proposal for Mr. Benini. He can supply a ton of product in the first year..."

"*What* product?"

"Don't be naïve, Mr. Shearing. Mr. Shir is based in Afghanistan. He has a great deal of experience exporting to the West. He can supply over a metric ton of premium product in the first year, giving Mr. Benini exclusive distribution rights."

He shook his head and a moment later laughed. "You have made some kind of mistake, Mr. Smith."

"Clearly. I understood Mr. Benini was the man to see about this kind of transaction. Mr. Shir will be very disappointed. Unfortunately, I fear you will be the scapegoat, having turned me away, albeit believing you were doing the right thing."

"Wait! Wait," he was still laughing, holding up his hands, "in the first place, who is this Mr. Shir> I mean, you know, you come in here out of the blue... What am I supposed to think? At least give me some kind of background."

I leaned forward and spoke very deliberately. "Mr. Shir is a very powerful man in Afghanistan. You understand what that means? He is a farmer, with thousands of hectares of land which he devotes to the cultivation of crops he knows he can sell in the West at very high prices. And believe me, Mr. Shearing, if Mr. Benini does not want to work with Mr. Shir, I can find a hundred in this city who will."

"No, now wait," he gave another little laugh, "let's not be hasty. That is not what I said. All we need here is a little communication. It's just this approach—" He gestured at me with both hands. "We don't usually do things this way in New York. Look, how about we start over? Coffee?"

I smiled. "Coffee would be nice."

He called Stella on his intercom and told her, "Coffee for two,

Stella." Then to me he said, "So, let's start at the beginning. Who, exactly, is Fateh Shir?"

"You're recording this conversation."

He opened his mouth, paused and let out a single, small laugh. "A precaution all attorneys take."

"And a definite limitation on the conversation we can have. However, I am sure that if you make discreet inquiries you will find that Fateh Shir is a man of some influence in Afghanistan. He is well respected by the Taliban, which as I am sure you will appreciate, is important these days. However, he also has channels of communication open with the West. He sometimes acts as a mediator, and in exchange for this certain Western governments allow him privileged trading conditions."

"I see." He nodded a few times. "And this product he wants to import into the United States is...?"

I raised an eyebrow at him. "Seriously?" I shook my head. "It is a crude product, sold in bulk, which can then be modified on receipt, and used in making various other products. We estimate its...," I paused and smiled, "*resale* value to be in the region of twelve hundred million dollars."

His jaw actually sagged. "Are you kidding me? *Twelve hundred million dollars?*"

I made a face that said I felt pain. "I think perhaps we have made a mistake. I think perhaps your outfit is not suited to this deal."

I labored the word "outfit" and made it as patronizing as I could. He was already shaking his head and waving his hands at me. "No, no, nonono! Please, sit, we can do this, I assure you. We are extremely professional and I *know* that Mr. Benini is just going to *love* this proposal. It's just, the number, it kind of took me by surprise."

The door opened and Stella came in with a tray of coffee which she set on the desk. I winked at her like I'd seen people like Robert de Niro do in movies about the mob. "Thanks, doll."

She left without answering. He poured coffee and handed me a cup. As I took it I spoke.

"I would suggest, Mr. Shearing, that you take a day to discuss our proposal with Mr. Benini. Make whatever inquiries you feel are necessary, and contact me. Say, sometime tomorrow evening? Then, if you are still keen to go ahead, we will arrange a meeting in a neutral place where there are no recording devices. Then I will be able to give you the full details of the product, method of shipping, distribution, et cetera."

"That sounds just fine. I was going to suggest it myself. Now, uh, will Mr. Shir be attending the meeting?"

"Mr. Shir cannot leave Afghanistan, Mr. Shearing. But you can think of me as Mr. Shir, multiplied in space and time. What I say goes."

He nodded a little more than was strictly necessary. "Of course, of course."

I reached in my pocket and pulled out one of the cards the colonel had prepared for me. I flipped it across the table to him.

"Call me tomorrow. I'll be waiting."

I stood and left the office, conscious of Stella's eyes on my back all the way to the door. The bored receptionist didn't look up.

I WASN'T ALL that surprised when I got home to see Angel sitting on the stoop. I glanced at my watch and saw it was shortly before one. I parked, killed the engine and smiled up at her.

"Hey, you. How you doing?"

I closed the soft-top, climbed out and mounted the steps to where she was sitting. The swelling had gone down on her lip and her eye and the cream was doing a decent job of hiding the bruises. She watched me a moment, but she wasn't smiling.

"I got a call this morning," she said.

I unlocked the door and she stood and followed me in.

"From a firm of brokers?"

"Yes. They wanted me to go in and sign some papers."

"And did you?"

"I wasn't going to, but in the end I did."

I closed the front door behind her, opened the door to the living room and followed her in. She stood looking around for a moment, with her back to the window and her face in shadow.

"You want a drink?"

"Have you got a Coke?"

"No." I smiled. "But I have some freshly squeezed pineapple juice."

I went to the kitchen and she leaned on the doorjamb, watching me while I poured it. As I handed it to her she asked me, "Who are you? What am I getting into by accepting this money?"

She sat at the kitchen table and I leaned my ass against the sink.

"Nothing."

"Nothing? That's hard to believe."

I thought for a moment, wondering how much I could tell her; how much I should tell her.

"I used to be in special forces. Now I am a kind of security consultant. I've made a lot of money in my time, one way and another. I have seen a lot of bad stuff. At times I have had to do bad stuff, and that has made me want, now, to do the right thing in life. Now that I can. That's a thumbnail sketch of me. What are you getting into?" I shrugged. "If you're smart you're not getting into anything. You are getting out of a mess. When I spoke to John Martinez I was able to scare the bejaysus out of him, and he agreed to make reparation for what he had done to you. I arranged to have that money invested..."

"How much money, Harry?"

"Five hundred thousand dollars. He had it in a sports bag in his wardrobe. The proceeds of his drugs sales. And you know what he was going to do with them? He was going to invest them in more drugs so he could destroy more lives with them."

"So you took the money?"

"No, he gave it to me, to give to you. So I handed it over to a bunch of brokers for them to invest it on your behalf. I did that because I knew that you would not accept half a million bucks' worth of blood money in a sports bag. But the money is yours, it's in your name, and you can take the capital any time you like."

She stared at the table for a while. Then she asked me, "And what do I have to do for this money? Again, what am I getting myself into? What are the strings?"

I gave a small snort of a laugh. "How old are you, Angel?"

"Twenty-three."

"Then let me make this very clear for you. You don't have to do anything, and by accepting that money you are not getting yourself into anything. There are no strings. My advice is, use it to go to college, get a degree and build a career in something you love doing. And that is *all* I ask of you, to generate some happiness and some joy. If you want to use it to go around the world and meet gurus, do that. If you want to start a company selling Mongolian rugs, do that. Just so long as you are happy doing it."

She was quiet for a long while, staring at her hands on the table, chewing her lip. Then she looked up at me. "I went to see Johnny, after I had left the brokers. I couldn't understand how he could have done this. I was..." She gave her head tiny shakes and let out an exasperated laugh. "I was in shock. It didn't make sense. But when I got there the place was crawling with cops. They wanted to know if I knew him. I said I had eaten there a few times. They told me he'd been murdered. Did you murder him, Harry?"

"No, Angel, I didn't murder him." I wasn't lying to her. As far as I was concerned I had executed him. "I scared the living daylights out of him, but I did not murder him. He gave me the money and I left."

"It's one hell of a coincidence, isn't it? I don't want that money if you murdered him for it."

"No." I shook my head. "It's not such a big coincidence at all, Angel. He was trafficking drugs, which means he was under an obligation to buy a certain amount every month from his suppliers. If he defaulted on that, they could well have killed him as a punishment and a warning to others. That's the way they operate. He was a dirty bastard living in a dirty world, Angel. Neither you nor I can be responsible for what happened to him."

She took a deep breath and sighed.

"I'm not a murderer, Angel."

"What about the boy who attacked me?"

"I think I broke his jaw, and I damaged his hand so he'd never use a knife again to hurt innocent people. I could have killed him in self-defense, but I didn't."

"I'm sorry. I must seem very ungrateful."

"No, you're being cautious and smart, and that's a good thing. So now you need to think about what you're going to do with your life. Make some smart choices."

"Gosh." She averted her eyes. "I've never been in *that* position before. Are you..." She trailed off and laid her hands on the tabletop, watching them like they might suddenly do something. "Now that you've done your good deed, are you just going to disappear?"

She mistook my hesitation and gave an ironic smile. "I figured as much."

"No, Angel, listen. I am not going to disappear. I gave you my card, remember? I want you to stay in touch, and I want to help you wherever I can. But sometimes I have to go away on a job. I never know when that is going to happen, or how long I'll be away. As long as you're aware of that, I'm here to help you if I can."

She sagged. "God, I am such a jerk. I'm sorry. You're so kind and generous, and it's like I'm complaining, saying it's not enough." An idea seemed to pop into her head and her face lit up. I realized then for the first time that she was actually beautiful. "Hey, when my face heals up, will you let me take you out to dinner, as a thank you?"

I laughed. "I'd like that." I gestured at the garden through the window behind me. "In the meantime, if you're in the mood, we can make a barbeque tonight in my backyard, crack some beers, talk."

"OK." Her eyes were bright and I felt glad suddenly that I had helped her. She stood and grinned. "I'm going to go and buy some clothes. What time do you want me back?"

I laughed. "Today is my day off. So you come back whenever you like."

I stood at the door and watched her run down the stairs and wave as she reached the bottom. A moment later she was gone, walking toward 5th Avenue.

SEVEN

SHE CAME BACK AT SEVEN. WE HAD A BARBEQUE AND A few beers in the backyard. We didn't talk about her future, her career or her money. We talked about just about everything else though, and at eleven thirty she insisted on getting a cab and going home. As I watched the red taillights pull away I wondered again what the hell I was doing. She had asked me what she was getting into, and I was asking myself the same question. I reassured myself that as soon as she was settled and went to college, she'd find a nice guy, make a life for herself and settle down. There was more than ten years between us, she was young and very naïve, and I was old—in spirit if not in body—and had left "experienced" so far behind I couldn't remember how to spell it anymore.

But what the hell, I told myself as I closed the door, she was fun to be with and it was nice to be helping somebody for a change, instead of blowing their brains out or severing their carotid artery. She was a friend, a protégé even. It didn't have to be "getting into" something. Did it?

I had a nightcap in the living room and made my way up to my bedroom at the top of the house. When I got there the window was open, a cool breeze was wafting in and there was a note on my pillow. It had been printed on an inkjet.

WHAT ARE YOU DOING, Harry? Do you really think this paternalistic, male chauvinist act of yours can wash your hands of all the blood they have on them? Do you think this act of egotism masquerading as kindness can mitigate the enormity of your crime? You are wrong. I watched you, lusting after your victim, and you disgust me. The clock is ticking. You will pay, as you must.

I DROPPED the note and ran. I bounded up the stairs to the attic. Both deadbolts were in place. I rammed them back and burst open the door, slammed on the light and bolted up the last few steps into the attic space. It was empty. The skylight was closed and sealed on the inside, as I had left it. I stood, staring around, my heart pounding and my mind reeling.

After a time I switched off the lights, closed and locked the door and went back to my bedroom. I poked my head out the window, looked down and saw what I knew I was going to see: a sheer wall not even a monkey could climb.

How had the son of a bitch got in? He must have picked the lock while I was out in the morning and waited up in the attic until he heard us in the backyard. Then the words struck me: "I watched you, lusting after your victim." So he had watched us in the backyard, but could not have known till then that Angel would be with me. So how then had he printed the note? He had either printed it before coming, in which case he could not have known she was going to have dinner with me, or he printed it while he was here, which was absurd.

I went to my study. The door was locked and when I opened it there was no indication my printer had been used, besides which it was a cheap, fifty-bucks model that made a noise, and he would have risked being heard.

It didn't make any sense. Either this guy was carrying around a portable printer, or he was referring to something else when he said he had seen me lusting after my victim. Either way, one thing was making me real nervous, and that was the ease with which this son of a bitch was getting in and out of my house.

I pulled on my jacket, slipped my P226 in my waistband behind my back and stepped out onto the stoop. I could see the car the brigadier had put on the house about thirty paces away on the far side of the road. I scanned up and down, didn't see anybody and trotted down the steps and along the far sidewalk until I came level with the car. I tapped on the glass. Nothing happened. For a moment I wondered if I'd got the wrong car. The streetlamp overhead had turned the windshield black with an orange glare, so I couldn't see inside. I tried the handle and the door opened.

They were there, both of them. The guy on the far side of the driver was staring at me with his mouth open. The driver was staring at the speedometer like it was his favorite toy. Each of them had a nice, neat red and black hole in the center of their foreheads. I didn't need forensics to tell me they were .22s. He would have used a semiautomatic with a suppressor, so the shell casings might just show up on the sidewalk or under the car, but they'd be as clean as Russian laundry. This guy probably spent more time in his surgical gloves than he did in his shorts.

I closed the door, hunkered down and searched the curb. I wasn't surprised to find zero shell casings. I called the brigadier, with the uneasy feeling I was being watched. I stepped back into the shadows of the tree beside the car and the brigadier answered.

"Harry."

"Your two guys who were keeping an eye on things?"

"Yes. What about them?"

"They won't be going home for Christmas."

He was silent for five long seconds. "Where are you?"

"Beside the car. But there's more."

"Tell me."

"Angel came over for a barbeque."

"I know. She was seen going in."

"The guy was in the house all that time. He left a note on my bed. She left in a taxi. I'm afraid he might go after her."

"This is why you should not have started a relationship with her. We'll discuss that later. This is going to derail the job. Stay with the car. Don't let anyone go near it. I'll have a tow truck there in ten minutes."

"Sir, send a car to her address. She does not deserve to pay for my mistakes."

He grunted and hung up.

I called her. While it rang a cold wind blew down the back of my neck and made me shudder. She answered on the fifth ring. A little drunk from just a couple of beers.

"You missing me already?"

I laughed, looking at the amorphous shapes of the two guys who sat dead in the car.

"Yeah, I just wanted to make sure you got home all right."

"Yes, daddy." A short pause, then, "You don't have to be my daddy, you know."

"I know."

"You only got one daddy, and one mommy. Anyone else is masquerading."

"I'm not your daddy, and I am not masquerading."

I was scanning the street, listening hard to the tiny sounds behind her voice. She sounded sleepy.

"No." She gave a silly laugh. "Or you'd be ten when you had me! I'm going to go to sleep now, Harry. You're a nice man and I like you. And you don't have to..." She took a deep breath and went silent. For a moment I felt the hot jolt of horror, thinking she'd stopped breathing, but then I heard the comfortable sound of soft snoring, and hung up.

Ten minutes passed and a tow-truck rolled up. They didn't acknowledge me and I didn't acknowledge them. We hadn't seen each other. I walked quickly away and returned to my house.

I bunched up pillows in my bed and covered them with the quilt, then went down to the living room, pushed one of the armchairs into the darkest corner and spent the night there without sleeping, with the Sig in my lap, fighting the impulse to go and check on Angel. I knew, as the brigadier knew, that the most dangerous thing for her right now was my attention.

At eight AM I called her from the secure line I used to call COBRA. It was something I shouldn't have done, but I knew I couldn't go to her and I couldn't call her on a regular line, so I made a once off exception. She answered with a pillow voice after the fifth ring, and I took a deep, silent breath of relief.

"Good morning, sleepyhead. How are you feeling?"

She made a sleepy noise and I heard her turn over. "I don't drink. How many beers did I have?"

"Four, but who's counting?"

"My head and my belly, for two."

"You know the best cure for a hangover?"

You could tell she was talking with her eyes still closed. "No, this is my first hangover, and it's your fault."

I felt a hot, inexplicable jolt of excitement in my belly and fought it down. I had remembered something I'd read once about the best cure for a hangover being a morning romp in bed. I pushed the thought away, but said, "Well, the second best is sleep. A high-protein breakfast and then a good sleep. You'll feel as good as new by midday."

"OK." A sleepy pause and then, "Harry?"

"Yup."

"What is the *best* cure for a hangover?"

"What I just said. I was joking." I was babbling and I knew it. "I was just remembering something from the army. Not appropriate for nice young ladies."

"Don't patronize me, daddy. I don't like being patronized."

"OK, the best cure is, don't sober up."

"Ugh, I don't like that one. I'll go with second best."

"Good. OK, it's early. You go back to sleep and I'll check up on you this afternoon."

"OK. And, Harry?"

"Yeah?"

"You're cute. Thanks."

I hung up and sat feeling troubled for a while. There was no word from the brigadier and no word from the colonel. I went down to the gym and spent a couple of hours working out and speed training on the sack. At eleven AM my phone rang.

I dried my face with a towel and grabbed the phone.

"Yeah."

"Mr. Smith?"

"Yes."

"This is Colin Shearing. I spent the evening with Mr. Benini last night, discussing your proposal. And I have to tell you that this morning we conducted a few preliminary background checks."

"So?"

"So Mr. Benini would like to meet you."

"Where and when?"

"Are you free today?"

"Let me check."

I took a stroll around the gym, did fifty push-ups, drank some water and strolled back.

"What time?"

"Say in a couple of hours?"

I sighed like that was a pain in the ass and said, "Yeah, OK. Where?"

"Mr. Benini's house in Pelham. It's..."

"I know where it is."

I had a hot shower followed by a cold one, then I went and had a pot of strong black coffee and some rye toast. I dressed, slipped my Sig Sauer under my arm and my Fairbairn and Sykes into my boot. Then I made my way down to the TVR.

It took a little less than half an hour to get there via the I-87 and the Bruckner Expressway. Pelham Manor was a green, leafy neighborhood with more trees than houses, and the Esplanade was a broad, quiet street with nothing in it but large houses surrounded by large trees. As I pulled up outside the sprawling manor, I saw the entrance gate was open and there was a guy in a double-breasted suit and heavy shades waiting for me. He waved me in and as I stopped at the front door, the gate behind me started to slide shut.

I climbed out of the car and he nodded at me. He was in his thirties and looked like he knew his way around a difficult situation.

"Nice ride."

"Thanks."

"European?"

"British."

"I gotta frisk you."

"OK, you'll find I have a Sig, P226, and a knife in my boot. I never leave home without them."

"You can collect them on your way out. And I still gotta frisk you."

I shook my head. "It was nice talking to you. Tell Mr. Benini if he wants to discuss business he can come and see me next time he's in Manhattan."

"Come on!" He spread his hands and lifted his shoulders. It was very Italian. "Be reasonable. I can't let you in the house with a piece and a blade."

"You don't have to. He does. Listen, I haven't got time to waste. Tell your boss I'm here, I carry a piece and a knife and I don't plan to hand them over. He can have six guys on me and a camera crew while we talk. I don't give a damn. I don't let go of my piece. Make the call or open the gate."

He sighed and pulled a small radio from his pocket.

"Hey, Boss. The guy is here. He has a Sig Sauer semiautomatic under his arm and a knife in his boot. He says he don't go nowhere without them, and if you won't let him in you have to go see him in Manhattan."

Among the static I heard "*Porca miseria!*" a few times followed by snatches of "*Porca puttana!...a morire ammazzato!... a pigliare in culo!... Coglione!...è uno stronzo pezzo di merda!*"

It went on like that for a while as the guy in the suit winced. I was about to tell him to open the gate for me when he said, "*Va benne,*" and turned to me. "OK, but if you put your hand inside your jacket, we'll be using you to drain spaghetti."

"Visual."

He led me through a house that was trying too hard to tell you just how powerful its owner was. As we passed through marble halls and courtyards, I never really knew whether to expect a guy in a sharp Italian suit and a trilby, or a guy in a toga with a scroll under his arm. We came eventually to an annex to the house with its own pool, set in a well-tended lawn and surrounded by tall cypress trees. The guy in the suit, who said his name was Tony and he preferred Italian cars to British ones, knocked on the door. He opened it and leaned in.

"Hey, Boss, the guy is here."

He jerked his head at me and said, "Go right on in."

It was a big room, more a library than a study or an office. The walls were lined floor to ceiling with leather-bound books on dark wood shelves. There was a fire burning in the grate and Marco Benini was sitting behind a big, mahogany desk that looked at least three hundred years old. He had his hands clenched into a double fist, like he was praying, and his chin resting on his knuckles while he regarded me with slightly yellow eyes.

There were three other men in the room. They were all wearing off the peg Armani suits and they all looked dangerous. Tony closed the door behind me and for a moment I was acutely aware that if they decided to kill me right then, I had an ice cube's chance in a supernova of getting out alive.

Mr. Benini sighed and stood. He forced something like a genial smile onto his face and reached out both hands. "Mr.

Smith, you are welcome in my home. Do you object to shaking hands?"

I said I didn't and we shook. He gestured me to a big, leather chair opposite his. He talked as we sat.

"All this COVID pandemic bullshit. They made it, you know? It was a joint Chinese-American venture in Hunan. I know the guy who devised it. The cure...," he paused, sighed, studied my eyes, "...is more dangerous than the illness."

"It's often the way."

"An aperitif? Sherry? Martini?"

"A dry martini would be nice."

"Tony, fix us a couple of dry martinis. Something non-alcoholic for you and the boys. Now, Mr. Smith, tell me about Fateh Shir, and explain to me why a good Catholic like me would want to do business with a fucking Taliban son of a bitch."

EIGHT

I SIPPED THE MARTINI AND SET IT CAREFULLY ON THE placemat in front of me on the desk.

"That is a damned good martini."

"It's what you should expect from an Italian New Yorker. Am I right?"

I nodded. "Let me answer your questions in reverse order. The answer to your second question is four simple words, each more beautiful than the last: twelve hundred million dollars."

I paused and he thought about it, seeing how the words increased progressively in beauty, then started to laugh and nod.

"Yeah, each more...yeah..." He pointed at me and looked over at his boys. "Million is better than a hundred, and dollars is the best of all. It's good. I like that."

"Fateh Shir is an Afghan. He works with, and cooperates with, the Taliban, though he is not Taliban himself. He also works with and cooperates with the American military and the US Government. Whenever there is negotiating to be done, covert business, dark ops—he is the go-to man. So, aside from being a source of a very valuable commodity, he is also a gateway to Afghanistan, which can be a very lucrative place."

He grunted, not yet impressed. "So what's this product you're selling?"

"Pure, premium, unprocessed opium of the very highest quality. He can provide at least a ton in the first year. Sold as opium, or converted into heroin, it has a potential street value of well over one thousand million dollars."

"It's too much." I almost stood up and made to leave, but waited instead, watching him. He shrugged like the notion was absurd. "Where do I store a ton of opium?"

I didn't hesitate. "In Afghanistan. Ship it over as and when you need it. He's not going to screw you. Aside from the fact that his reputation is really important to him, he needs to sell this stuff. He will accommodate you. He has no problem storing the stuff. As and when you can shift it, you fly it to Papua New Guinea."

His eyebrows shot up and he stuck out his neck. "*Where?*"

I offered him a smart-ass smile. "Exactly. Mr. Shir has an especially modified plane for long-distance flights. It stops over for refueling at Aek Godang Airport, in Janin Manahan, north Sumatra. He has longstanding friends in the government there. The plane refuels and flies on to the Maralina airstrip, in Maralina, Papua New Guinea. From there you can ship the stuff into Canada or the United States. You know better than anyone that customs is focused on the border with Mexico. Nobody thinks twice about stuff coming from Papua New Guinea. Look at your own reaction. You could bring it in by the container load. Nobody would check it. You could stuff it into hollow wooden carvings, native pottery, whatever. It's a cinch."

"What about processing it into heroin?"

"You can set up the operation there, in Maralina, or here, in the Rockies. Ship it to Seattle, process it in Colorado. You can also sell it as opium, without processing it. Opium is becoming more popular as a recreational drug."

"You got it all figured, huh?"

I tried not to look disdainful and failed. "It's not the first time we've done something like this."

He nodded a few times, trying to read my face. "We had a poke around. Nobody ever heard of you."

"I would hope not. I wouldn't be much use to Mr. Shir if I were famous."

"How much is this ton of opium going to cost me?"

"It's actually a little over a metric ton. It's twelve shipments of one hundred kilos, so you actually get one ton and two hundred Ks. That's going to be four million per shipment, and we are going to need the first payment up front."

He shook his head. "Four million? That is well above market price."

"Sure it is. Not only is it the best opium on the market, you are getting guaranteed delivery straight from Afghanistan, and virtually risk free."

"From a fucking Taliban I cannot hope to get at if he screws me over." He gestured at me with an open hand and an expression of contempt so deep you could breed extremophiles in it. "And a fucking nobody, nobody ever heard of."

I nodded. "Thank you." He leaned back in his chair, watching me, savoring his contempt like a fine cognac. I could have killed him there and then. I might have taken a couple of his boys too, but I didn't fancy making this my last job, and I was pretty sure he was bluffing. "You cleared up a doubt for me. I know Mr. Shir would not want to do business of this magnitude with a piece of shit who hasn't got the balls or the resources to risk four million bucks to make a billion. Apparently you are mid-level crap and you will never be much more. I think I'll be better off dealing with the Russians. The Italians seem to have lost their guts."

He had gone a deep shade of purple. I stood and his boys started closing on me. I pointed at him. "If one of these Italian queens touches me, you will be blown to kingdom come in the next few days on your way to Park Avenue. Your house will be firebombed and all your family will be slaughtered. Now, Mr.

Benini, are we done measuring dicks, or do you want to take it to the next level? I did not come here to waste time. I came here to negotiate. You want the deal, take it. You want to piss in the wind in a second-rate mansion in Pelham, it's your choice."

"OK!" He snarled. "Enough!"

"I hope it is. What goes down in this room stays in this room, but make no mistake, Benini. This is not spaghetti and violin cases. Your bulletproof limo is not going to keep you safe from these guys. They'll come into your house, gut your family and hang you from your balls with a piano wire. Am I getting through to you?"

I paused, but all he did was stare at me. I shrugged. "But play nice, and you can make a billion bucks in a year. I have worked for Mr. Shir for years now, and I can tell you he is a generous, loyal friend, with very useful friends in international banking, construction, shipping..." I smiled as I watched the greed melt his face. "It's a once in a lifetime chance. Don't blow it."

I took a step toward the door and stopped to turn back to him. "Call me. If I haven't heard from you in twenty-four hours I'll assume you're not interested. Then I'll have to decide how much of a liability you have become." I gave what you'd call a humorless laugh. "I'm figuring you have recorded this conversation, and that makes you a liability, right? Either way, if I don't hear from you, I will open a dialogue with the Russians." I paused again. "Do the smart thing, Benini." As an afterthought I added, "Next time, we meet on my terms."

I moved to the door. Tony was standing in front of it. He didn't look happy.

"You disrespected my uncle."

"Step aside, kid."

"I can't. You disrespected the boss."

I didn't take my eyes off him. "Benini. Tell your nephew to step aside. Let's keep this friendly."

The voice came from behind me. "Tony, let the man leave. We are negotiating."

"*Zio!* He insulted you and the *famiglia!*"

"Leave it!" And then more quietly. "*Avrai la tua occasione più tardi.*"

He'd get his chance later. Tony wagged a finger in my face. "Later, Smith."

"Keep your fingers in your pockets, kid, or you're liable to lose them."

Five minutes later I drove out of the Benini mansion with the comfortable feeling that the Hollywood Mafia were alive and well, and it was only a matter of time before I ran into Al Pacino talking like he had laryngitis, about how disappointed he was.

I got back to my house on East 128th, parked at the foot of my stoop and climbed out of the car. I had made it to the second step when I heard the voice behind me. It was a quiet, educated voice that carried authority.

"Mr. Bauer?"

I stopped and turned. He was fair and blue-eyed, in his mid-thirties. He had a good, though tired off-the-peg suit, good shoes that had been well worn and a face that was tired of waiting. By his shape and his carriage, he worked out a lot in the gym.

"Yeah."

He nodded at my front door. "Is this your house?"

I paused before answering, but couldn't think of any reason to lie.

"Yeah, why?"

He pointed at the TVR. "And this is your car?"

"That's a lot of questions, friend. Do you mind telling me how any of this is your business?"

"No." He reached inside his pocket and pulled out a leather wallet. He let the flap drop and I went back down the two steps I'd taken to have a look at it. I said, "Special Agent Alistair McDonald, from the Federal Bureau of Investigation." I handed back the badge. "Are you Scottish, Agent McDonald?"

"Mexican. You'd be surprised at how many Mexicans have Celtic names."

"Maybe I wouldn't. What interest has the FBI in my house and my car?"

"Were you at a bar recently on the corner of 1st Avenue and East 115th?"

"Johnny's Bar, yes I was. What of it?"

"Did you have an altercation with the owner?"

"I had an altercation with a kid in the bar who pulled a knife on me, and then I had an altercation with the owner."

"And you went there in your car." He gestured again at the TVR. "This TVR."

"That's what I am telling you, Agent McDonald, and I am being very patient waiting for you to tell me what this is all about."

"Mr. Bauer, I have to ask you, did you stab the young man in the hand, lacerating his tendons..."

"Yeah, and he's lucky I didn't kill him. I would have been justified in doing so. He pulled a knife on me and tried to kill me. Earlier that day I had watched him attempt to stab a young woman on Lenox and 125th, just outside the subway. Again, Agent McDonald, what has this to do with the Bureau?"

"Mr. John Martinez, the owner of the bar, with whom you had your altercation, was found murdered later that day. Your car was seen parked outside the establishment, and a man fitting your description was seen getting in to the car."

He looked at me like he had scored a point. I smiled like my patience was wearing real thin.

"Agent McDonald. My car, that car, would be noticed wherever it went. It would especially be noticed outside Johnny's Bar on 1st Avenue. So let me ask you, how many other cars were there that would *not* be noticed?" I paused but he didn't answer. I went on. "A man fitting my description was seen getting into the car. Any man getting into that car would be noticed. But let me ask you, yet again, how many men left the bar and got into BMWs, Fords and VWs, who were not noticed but might also fit my description?"

He still didn't say anything. He just waited, watching me.

"Let me explain something to you, Agent McDonald. I was eight years with the British Special Air Service, and they taught me to do one thing extremely well. They taught me to kill people. Do you know what the most important part of killing somebody is?"

His eyes had become frosted, and there was real dislike in his face. "Why don't you tell me, Mr. Bauer?"

"The most important part about killing somebody, is being able to get away unharmed and unnoticed. So I can guarantee that if I had gone to Johnny's Bar to kill him and his punk, I would not have gone in a TVR, nobody would have noticed me arrive or leave, and his punk associate would not be nursing a paralyzed hand now, he'd be on a deep six holiday to Hell, where he belongs."

He looked like a man making a concerted effort not to be impressed.

"Why *did* you go to Johnny's Bar, Mr. Bauer?"

"Because he had sent his punk to mug a young woman. I witnessed the attack. The girl wound up with a cut lip and a badly bruised face. If I had not intervened she'd probably have been stabbed to death. I talked to the girl and I decided I liked her. So I went to have a talk with Johnny and explain to him that it's not nice to send punks after naïve young girls. His punk attacked me with a knife and I showed extreme restraint in not ramming his knife up his ass. Now, I am going to ask you for the last time, Agent McDonald, what business is this of the FBI's? What I am asking you is, how is this a federal matter?"

"John Martinez was a drug trafficker who was bringing in narcotics from the Southwest, probably from Mexico. We are considering the possibility that you were paid to take him out. It's not unheard of for ex-special forces soldiers to take contracts."

"Believe me, McDonald, I'd have taken Johnny Martinez out for free. But you're barking up the wrong tree. I'm a professional, not an amateur. And you know what? I don't do that anymore."

He raised an eyebrow. "You did before?"

"Oh yeah." I laughed. "With the blessings of Her Majesty Queen Elizabeth II of England."

We stood staring at each other for a moment. Then he nodded briefly. "Thank you for your cooperation, sir."

As he turned to go I said, "McDonald, from Mexico. I once met a McDonald from Mexico, very briefly. I wonder if he was a relative of yours." He turned to look at me, but once again said nothing. I went on. "His first name was Gregorio. Gregorio McDonald. Family?"

He shook his head. "No, must be a different McDonald."

I watched him get into a cream Taurus and pull away. I climbed the steps again and let myself into the house. I searched it from top to bottom but found nothing out of place and called the brigadier.

"I might be wrong, but I think my stalker just introduced himself to me."

"Explain."

"I need you to make inquiries, find out if the Bureau's New York field office has a Special Agent Alistair McDonald investigating drug rings operating between the Southwest and New York."

"Is that who he claimed to be?"

"Yeah, and I think he might be related to Gregorio McDonald, a Mexican drug trafficker I handed over to Peter Rusanov at the Mescal Club just before I joined COBRA. I didn't kill him, but I may as well have. I killed his boys in the parking lot of the club. Then I handed Gregorio over to Rusanov. Gregorio wanted to take over the club and Rusanov obviously made an example of him. If this G man is related to him, he may well want to make an example of me."

"I'll make inquiries. I'll let you know what we find."

"Thanks."

I searched the house again from top to bottom and slipped

the six deadbolts into place: the attic, the front door and the back door. Then I settled in the living room to wait for my executioner.

NINE

My executioner didn't come, but at four PM my telephone rang. The screen told me it was Angel and my common sense told me not to answer. My common sense is a much neglected part of me. I pressed the green button.

"Hey, how's the hangover? Are you up yet?"

"Yeah, more or less. My hangover is better. I don't drink. Did I tell you? I'm a bit of a health freak."

"That's good."

"You're in pretty good shape yourself. You work out a lot?"

"Yeah."

"Maybe we could go running together some mornings."

Now was the time to tell her I was not somebody she should hang out with. So I said, "That could be fun. You ever practice any martial arts?"

"Some, Tae Kwon Do mainly. Wasn't much use to me the other day."

I offered her a grim laugh. "Martial arts are not quite the same as street fighting. If you like we could do some training together. Might be useful."

"I'd like that." A silent pause, then, "What are you doing this afternoon?"

"I have a job I have to take care of. I'll be tied up for a couple of days."

"Oh," a small laugh, "figuratively, right?"

"Figuratively. I hope. After that I'll have more free time."

"Harry, can I ask you a personal question?"

"You can ask. I can't promise I'll answer."

"Do you like me."

"Sure."

"No, I don't mean like that, like you can casually say, 'Yeah, sure I like you, kid.' I mean do you *like* me. Guys don't, usually. I'm not the kind of girl guys like."

"Well that's hard to believe, Angel. You're very attractive."

"You do like me, then?" Before I could answer she went on. "I think it's because I don't like guys of my age. I think they're shallow and inexperienced. I am attracted to slightly older men, who have lived and have life experience, like you. I am very drawn to you." She paused. I searched frantically for something to say. She asked me, "Are you drawn to me?"

The problem was, I told myself, that in some strange way I was, and I did not want to lie to her. The world had been cruel to this girl, and I did not want to be the guy who made it worse.

I took a deep breath, telling myself it was for her own good and her own safety, and with a burning pellet of crazy excitement in my gut I heard myself say the exact opposite of what I was thinking.

"Yes, Angel, I am drawn to you and I do find you attractive. But I have to tell you that it's a lot more complicated than you think."

"Complicated how? Is that an excuse because you don't want to hurt me?"

I looked out at the silent, still trees outside my window. She was too young, she was too naïve, she was too good. It would be like taking a white butterfly in your hands when they were covered in the blood and gore of a slaughter.

"No," I said simply. "I don't want to hurt you. But it is also complicated."

"That's what men say when they mean, 'You're not my type,' or 'I'm getting in too deep and I'm married.'"

I sighed. "I am no good at this kind of conversation, Angel. I can tell you I don't often lie. I like you, I am more attracted to you than I ought to be and that is affecting my judgment..."

I closed my eyes and told myself to shut up before I did or said something stupid that I would live to regret—like I hadn't already. But there was a definite, happy smile in her voice when she replied.

"I think that's the nicest thing anyone has ever said to me."

"You have to believe me, Angel, when I tell you that I am not a good man to be involved with. I can be a good friend to you, but you do not want to get too close."

"You want me to stay naïve and inexperienced all my life?"

"There are some experiences you don't need to have."

"Who decides that? You? Or me? Maybe I need the experiences you can give me. Maybe I need that intensity."

"I can't do this now, Angel. This job is not the kind of job I can be late on..."

She ignored me and spoke quietly in a voice that twisted my gut and made my heart pound, high up in my chest.

"And maybe you need to give that intensity to a naïve girl like me. Had you thought about that, Harry?"

"Stop, Angel. This is getting out of hand."

"OK." Her voice was small, fragile, vulnerable. "I'll be here, thinking of you. Please call me, Harry, when you have finished the job. I need to talk to you."

"I will."

I hung up and immediately felt the absence of her voice. I remembered my gigantic Kiwi sergeant scowling across the table in the pub with a glass of Bushmills in his hand.

"I've slept like a fuckin' babe in arms, with five hundred

ragheads three hundred yards away on the other side of a hill. But what five hundred bastards armed with AK47s can't do—rob me of my sleep—one slip of a girl with big vulnerable eyes can do in a fuckin' heartbeat. They turn intelligent men into idiots, and tough survivors into fuckin' suicides. That's women."

He had knocked back the whiskey and turned his attention to his Guinness, wagging a huge finger at me.

"And I'll tell you something else for free. The most dangerous woman is the good one. The innocent one. Because we have no defense against a good, innocent woman. A whore? You know where you stand with a whore. You can be mates, you're dealing in cash, you know where the lines are drawn. But a good, innocent woman, you..." He had frowned and shook his head. "You feel *obligated* to her. They play on your fuckin' conscience and they end up owning you. Give me a good brothel any day of the week."

I booked a suite at the Marriott Residence Inn, in the Bronx, and spent the rest of the day in my gym, working out and taking repeated hot and cold showers. As night fell I checked all my deadbolts, attic, front door and back, set my bed up to look like I was sleeping in it and spent the night in the living room again, with the Sig Sauer in my lap.

I allowed myself to sleep at six thirty AM and awoke four hours later at ten thirty. I had a cold shower, made strong black coffee and rye toast, and called Benini. The phone was answered by someone who sounded like he was pretending to have a cleft pallet.

"Nyuh. Mita B'nini'd wezidens."

"This is Mr. Smith, I'd like to speak to Mr. Benini."

"Hod'wine pweez."

There was a protracted silence and Benini's voice came on the line. I noticed a slight quiver of rage in it and figured he hadn't slept much.

"Mr. Smith, good morning."

"Have we decided to be sensible?"

"Don't patronize me, Mr. Smith. My patience has a limit, and you are reaching it fast."

"One o'clock in the afternoon at the Marriott New York Residence Inn, in the Bronx on Eastchester Road. You know it?"

"Yeah, I know it."

"Be there, and leave your attitude in Pelham."

"How do I know you're not a Fed? How do I know this isn't a setup?"

"Stop pissing in the wind, Benini. You're not the only one with patience issues. I've given you time to check me out and my principal. You know we're for real. Bring your boys along for the party. I don't give a damn. Now either you want the business or you don't. There is only one Fateh Shir, Benini, but guys like you in New York are a dime a dozen. Now stop wasting my time. Get with the program or get lost."

There was silence. He was having a hard time swallowing his ego. I sighed noisily.

"OK, forget it. My damage limitation team will be in touch..."

"No! Wait, goddammit! OK, the Marriott New York Residence Inn, the Bronx, on_Eastchester Road. I'll be there at one." A subtle change came over his voice. "You play hardball, Mr. Smith."

"That's how we get things done, Mr. Benini. You're in a different league now. I'll see you there."

I hung up and sat thinking. I could make the hit today. It would be risky, but it could be done. The textbook approach would be to gain his trust, arrange one more meeting and make the hit then, with minimized risk. But it was tempting to break the rules and shoot him today. A plastic bag with a muddy mush of chocolate, oil and whole meal flour would be enough to hold their attention long enough for me to pull the Maxim 9 and pop them. The deciding factor would be how many of his boys he brought with him.

I went to the kitchen and spent an hour experimenting with

cocoa, oil, flour and various other ingredients until I had a nasty goo that looked convincingly like raw opium. I wrapped a pound of it in film, and then put that into a transparent sandwich bag, which I in turn wrapped once more in transparent film. I put that in my attaché case on the off chance I might want to use it.

I cleaned and loaded my Maxim and strapped on my Fairbairn and Sykes around my ankle. Finally I went down to the TVR and drove to the Montefiori Wellness Center on Waters Place, in the Bronx and left my car in the parking lot there. Then I stepped out onto the road and hailed a cab. He dropped me at the Marriott ten minutes later and I collected the key to my suite on the top floor at twelve forty-five.

In the elevator I called Benini and told him the room number.

"Do not check at the desk. Just come straight on up."

They arrived twenty minutes later. Obviously his inquiries into Fateh Shir plus my bad attitude had done the trick because he arrived with just two boys, Tony and an older guy who'd had a bad case of acne forty years ago, when he was young.

I had my jacket off on the back of a chair, my Maxim in full view, and as I let them in I said to Benini, "You're welcome to scan the place for bugs and check me for a wire. My jacket is on the chair. I want you to feel comfortable. We are here to negotiate, not to fight with each other."

He stared at me through narrowed eyes, trying not to show surprise at my change of tone.

"I appreciate the gesture. Tony..." He jerked his chin at me, and as Tony checked me and my jacket for a wire, Berto, the older guy, went around the suite with a CAM 4G bug detector. Tony found nothing and eventually Berto shrugged and said, "It's all clear."

I gestured at the sofa and the chairs which were arranged around a coffee table in the middle of the floor.

"Mr. Benini, shall we sit?" We sat and I went on. "Mr. Shir is anxious that we should now start to build a relationship of trust and cooperation. In our business the risks are high, and friendship is a rare and valuable commodity. It is part of Mr. Shir's philosophy that if you screw your partner you can maybe make an extra hundred or two hundred million. But if you befriend your partner, the benefits can run into thousands of millions. He calls this, '*Ada' raghbatih alkhasa*,' literally it means to illuminate your own desire, but the meaning Mr. Shir gives it is that of an enlightened self-interest."

Benini spread his hands and shrugged. "That's a real nice sentiment. Let's take it a step at a time and see if the cooperation lives up to the philosophy."

I smiled agreeably, so that the implied threat was only slightly visible. "I am sure that with mutual effort and commitment, we will all benefit, Mr. Benini."

"So, where do we go from here?"

"We will need four million dollars in advance. It can be either in cash, or deposited into an offshore account. Following which the goods will be dispatched and arrive in New York in approximately one week."

He stared out the window from where he was sitting, nodded slowly a few times and then turned to look at me. "Four million bucks." I didn't say anything, but I could see the ill-repressed anger in his face. "Four million bucks," he said again.

I said, quietly, "It's the same figure I gave you yesterday. And as I told you yesterday, it has a street value more than twenty times that. We are talking about eighty to a hundred million dollars. I hope you don't feel you're being short-changed, Mr. Benini."

He licked his lips. He was having trouble believing the numbers. I knew how he felt.

"That's a lot of money."

"It's pure opium. You don't have to go through a long line of middlemen. You set up your own lab in the Rockies and you process it into pure heroin, then you cut it and you distribute it. All the profits are for you. You win and we win."

"OK, suppose I agree. I am going to part with four million

bucks—that's not the kind of cash you just have lying around—and what guarantee do I have that my dope is going to show up?"

"Mr. Shir's reputation should be guarantee enough."

He laughed a laugh rich in nicotine. "Yeah, maybe in Afghanistan, but not in New York. I have been working this market for a long time, Mr. Smith, and nobody hands over the money without either receiving the goods, or some damn good guarantee that the goods will arrive."

My mind went to my attaché case sitting on the bed in the bedroom. It would be easy to bring it in and dump the bag of slime in front of him. All their eyes would be on it. Pure opium is not something you see every day, even in the drugs trade. I would have a full four seconds to take all three of them out.

But then there were the spoils of war that the brigadier was so fond of talking about. He seemed to be accepting the price tag of four million bucks, and that wasn't something to be sneered at. I sighed.

"OK, Mr. Benini. Clearly, a hundred kilos of pure opium is not something I can bring along to a Marriott hotel suite. But I can bring you, say, four kilos as a goodwill gesture, and so that you can see the quality of the product. You make the transfer, or hand over the cash, and we move forward on the shipment. Will that satisfy you?"

He thought about it a moment, "Four Ks? That's like nine pounds, right?"

I nodded. "Eight point eight, which you will then, of course, cut."

He was calculating in his mind and he knew he could make up a good part of his four million on the sample alone. "Yeah," he said, "yeah, that would be OK."

"I will call you with the location in the next few hours and arrange a meeting for either tomorrow or the day after. Will you pay cash or make a transfer to an account in Belize?"

He had another brief think and said, "I'll make a transfer to your bank in Belize."

I looked at him for a long moment, thinking that he had bought himself a few extra hours of life, and wondering how he was going to spend them. I hoped I hadn't blown my chance at executing the job. I had a sneaking bad feeling, and was trying not to regret my decision.

"Good," I said at last. "Mr. Shir will be very pleased, I am sure."

TEN

They left and I sat for a while in the bedroom staring at the near empty attaché case with its brick of brown goo. Eventually I took the case down to my car and drove slowly back toward Manhattan. On the way I called the brigadier. When he answered I told him.

"I should discuss this with the colonel. But as it seems we are all fifteen again, I'll have to discuss it with you, sir."

"Give her a little time, Harry. What do you need?"

"I need a safe house where I can have the final meeting with Benini. It needs to be remote, but not so far away he'll become suspicious."

He grunted, then said, "Long Island, Montauk. We have a cottage out there on the beach. Hero's Cottage, three miles past Lake Montauk, on the Old Montauk Highway."

"That's good. There's something else I need. I need four kilos of high-grade, pure opium."

"How soon?"

"Yesterday should be soon enough."

"Understood."

"And a pound of C4."

"Just as well you spoke to me then, instead of the colonel, isn't it? I thought we were going to keep this low key. I am not sure I am very happy about explosions going off at the cottage."

"I'm not going to blow anything up, sir. I just need to create a small distraction." I told him what I planned to do and he listened carefully.

"We don't want collateral damage, Harry, and that includes the five-hundred-thousand-dollar cottage."

"With all due respect, sir. That's what I told you."

"Fair enough. Anything else?"

"Yeah, what happened with this Fed who came to see me, McDonald?"

"Yes, I'm glad you brought that up. The Bureau's New York field office has no record of a Special Agent Alistair McDonald. So we looked into Gregorio McDonald and found that he did have a son. In fact he had seven sons. Two of them were legitimate, with his wife Olga Maria, three were with prostitutes who worked in his clubs and two more with his live-in mistress. None of them was called Alistair. They all had Mexican names."

I thought about it as I cruised along the Bruckner Expressway, headed west. "Have you got all this in a report?"

"Yes, there are more details. I'll have it sent to you. It's preliminary, obviously, but you should have a careful look."

"Thanks. What about local law enforcement?"

"We're looking into that. Obviously that will take a little longer."

"Sure. When can I collect the stuff?"

"Go directly to the cottage this afternoon. You'll find everything you need there. I'll FedEx the key to you as soon as the place is ready."

I thanked him and hung up.

When I got to James Baldwin Place and parked outside my house, I noticed a car on the other side of the road. It was the familiar, nondescript Ford Taurus and I could make out the vague figure of a man behind the wheel. By the time I'd started to climb the steps to my door I could hear his shoes crossing the blacktop.

So I stopped and turned. McDonald climbed the steps and stood level with me. I noticed again that despite his unremarkable appearance he was athletic in build. He was the most dangerous kind of gray man. Before he could speak I said, "You're a liar, McDonald."

"Seems to me you're in something of a glass house, Mr. Bauer. You shouldn't be throwing stones."

"It's an offence to impersonate a federal officer."

"As with all criminal laws, the offence is to be proven guilty. I think you'd have some difficulty proving I did that."

"What do you want, McDonald?"

His voice was quiet—too quiet. It was insidious and got inside you, like a cold breeze on a frosty night. He smiled. "I just want to do my job."

"So go do it and leave me alone."

"That's a contradiction in terms, Mr. Bauer. You see, you are my job. I aim to prove that you are one of New York's most prolific contract killers."

I smiled. Then I threw back my head and laughed. "You're a freelance investigative reporter. You heard about my background in special forces, you saw I made some money, and your nasty, envious little soul made you want to expose me for the murdering bastard I am. Am I close?"

"Let's say you are. Would you grant me an interview?"

I climbed the stoop the rest of the way to the front door, shoved the key in the lock and opened the door. Then I turned. "Sure, why not? You have fifteen minutes. Then I have to go and arrange a hit."

I made the comment with heavy irony, but he watched me with expressionless eyes, then climbed the last few stairs and entered the hall. I closed the door and we stood facing each other.

"Who are you?"

"I told you. My name is Alistair McDonald."

"Why are you stalking me?"

"I'm not stalking you, Mr. Bauer. I am investigating you."

"Why?"

I have already told you that, too. Because I aim to prove you are a professional killer. Let me ask you something, Mr. Bauer. Is my life at risk right now?"

There was no fear in his eyes. He was cool and rock steady. I asked him:

"Is mine?"

"Yes. You will either die in the next couple of days, or you will spend the rest of your life behind bars. Either way, what you know as life is coming to an end."

I narrowed my eyes, like I was trying to penetrate his skull. "*Why?* And don't give me your evasive bullshit. Why would you give a damn about me? Why go to all this trouble and effort? What have you got against me? What the hell do you think you know about me?"

The smile was slow. It moved up from his lips, through his cheeks until it reached his eyes. It was a cruel smile. There was no room in it for compassion or pity. It was a smile of secret, ruthless triumph.

"What do I think I know? I don't know how to begin to answer that, Mr. Bauer. Let me start by saying I don't *think* I know anything. I know what I know. I know you are a man without conscience. I know you are a man without pity. I know that you kill people without consideration and without thought. And I know you have not even the justification of vengeance or outrage. You are doing it coldly, for money, to satisfy your masters. And I know that that puts you among the lowest forms of humanity."

I scowled. "Why? How? How do you know that? Where did you get that information?" He smiled, enjoying my frustration, and drove me to ask the question. "Are you related to Gregorio McDonald? Was he your father?"

His smile, still cold and cruel, broadened. "So you admit it."

"I don't admit a goddamned thing. I am asking you if he was your father. Keep pushing, pal, and I'm going to drag you upstairs and dangle you from the window till you tell me who the hell you are!"

It didn't shake him. "And you ask me where I get my information from." He gave his head a small shake. "All I have to do is observe you. You're a walking charnel house. Wherever you go people die, butchered by you."

"For the last time, goddammit! Based on what? You can't just throw accusations at me and act like it's a damned given that they're true! What's your evidence? Where's your proof? And for that matter, what damned right have you got to be stalking me in the first place?"

"It's my job."

"Bullshit! I checked with the Feds and they've never heard of you."

"Yeah? What a surprise. I talk to them quite often."

I took a step toward him, but he raised a finger and made a quiet, "Ah!" With his left hand he reached in his breast pocket and pulled out a leather wallet which he dropped open. It said he was Detective Alistair McDonald of the New York Police Department.

I snarled, "Another phony badge?"

He shook his head. "The NYPD has been looking at you since you moved here from the Bronx. That was quite a move: pokey little cottage on the water, to a big, beautiful brownstone in Manhattan, just a few blocks from the park. Looks like fortune smiled on you, huh, Harry?"

"You have no grounds to investigate me."

"Really? Where were you today? You booked a room in a hotel in the Bronx. Were you feeling nostalgic? And for just one night. A night you didn't even spend there. That seems to me to be odd behavior, wouldn't you agree, Harry?"

"That is none of your goddamn business. As far as I know, McDonald, behaving oddly is not yet a crime."

He ignored me. "It was quite a coincidence. You used the room for a little more than an hour, and you know who turned up during that hour?" I went cold inside. He saw it and smiled. "Mr. Marco Benini and two of his thugs. He's a man much like you, Harry. Everybody knows he's a killer, but nobody has been able to prove it—yet."

I spoke very quietly. "Your problem, McDonald, is that you have become obsessed, because you believe I killed Gregorio McDonald. What was he, your father? Whatever your relationship was, when he died you pinned it on me. But you're wrong. I was just the doorman that night. And if you keep letting that obsession drive you, you are going to wind up in deep trouble."

He frowned. "Really? What kind of trouble would that be, Harry? You wouldn't be threatening me, would you?"

I spoke through gritted teeth. "The man who killed Gregorio McDonald was Peter Rusanov. I was not even there. I was sent home. McDonald had turned up with a van full of punks with AK47s. He was going to make a massacre in that club!"

"Keep talking, Harry." He took a step closer, so he was just a couple of inches away, looking straight in my eyes. "But whatever you say, you are responsible for Gregorio McDonald's death, just as though you had wielded the machete yourself. And the problem I have with going after Peter Rusanov, Harry, is that curiously enough, he happens to be dead too."

"You know I'm going to call the 32nd Precinct, and the 40th, and if you're not on their staff, the next time I see you I am going to exercise my right to protect myself."

He gave a small laugh. "Sure, Harry, everyone has a right to defend themselves. Even monsters like you. I'll look forward to it. You take it easy, now." He paused at the door and looked back at me. "Have a shot to calm yourself down. You like the expensive stuff, don't you? The Macallan? Have a nice evening."

He stepped out and I followed him out to the stoop just as a FedEx biker rolled up. McDonald stopped at his car and watched, smiling, as the biker ran up the steps and handed me a large envelope. I signed for it and the biker left. McDonald climbed in his car and I watched him drive away.

When he was gone I examined the house. I didn't find anything out of the ordinary. So I went out, took a cab to a shopping mall in the Bronx, bought a burner and called the brigadier.

"Why are you calling from this number?"

"We have got a big problem."

"Be precise and be brief."

"Alistair McDonald was waiting for me when I got back. He had followed me to my meeting with Benini. He knew I had booked a room at the Hyatt. He saw Benini arrive while I was there and put two and two together. He also accused me of killing Gregorio McDonald and said he knew I was a paid killer. He does not know who I work for. He showed me a different badge this time and claimed to be a detective with the NYPD. If he's in my precinct, that's the 32nd. If it's where McDonald was killed, it's the 40th. I need to know if he's a real cop."

He was silent for a long moment. Then, "It's too soon to decide whether to abort. I need to make inquiries. If he is not a policeman, then he somehow has access to a great deal of information."

I cut in. "He is obviously a trained, and highly experienced investigator. McDonald may not be his name. He may have used it simply to rattle me. The question is, what does he want?"

"He's a damned sight more than an experienced investigator, Harry. He has killed two of our men and broken into your house multiple times without your noticing. He was living in my attic, and you didn't know. You know how that works, Harry."

I scowled. "*What?*"

"What is our motto?"

I frowned, thinking. "Who Dares Wins."

"You have seen that a hundred times on operations. Sometimes, the sheer reckless courage of a person who no longer gives a damn can carry them twice as far as a person with the best training in the world. He may well be highly trained and experienced. But more than that, he doesn't care about the risks."

I thought about it. "Yeah, you may be right. This guy is cool. He is not afraid."

"All right. You'll see a van down the road from your house when you get home. We'll be watching and listening. These are not just pros like the other two, Harry. These are blades." Blades were what we called members of the Regiment. "The corporal is one of our best men. They know what they are doing. No one is going to take them out. So go home, relax, and prepare for the next meeting with Benini. I'm going to make inquiries. If we need to abort you'll be the first to know. Until then, the operation is a go. You got the report?"

"OK. Yeah, I got it. Oh, one more thing. Have someone drop me off a Land Rover for tomorrow. I don't want to use the TVR. It's not exactly subtle."

I hung up, dumped the burner and made my way home by train, bus and taxi, making it virtually impossible for anyone except the whole of the KGB en force to follow me. At six PM FedEx delivered a small package which turned out to be the key to the cottage on Long Island. I decided to go see the place in the morning, and at six thirty I pulled a steak from the fridge and started heating a cast-iron pan with sunflower oil. I made some salad to keep my conscience happy and when the pan was frighteningly hot I sprinkled coarse salt on the meat and prepared to drop it on the searing iron.

Then the doorbell rang. I sighed and waited, hoping it wouldn't ring again. It did, insistently. I removed the pan and crossed the hall to the door. I looked through the spyhole and saw it was Angel. I felt a hot jolt of pleasure which was all twisted up with anxiety.

I opened the door. It wasn't cold but she had a woolen hat on and a scarf and gloves.

"You're dressed for three months' time."

She stared at me a moment before speaking. "I am so sorry to be a pain, Harry. I'll go if you want me to."

"No. Don't be silly. Come on in. What's the problem?"

"I'm scared."

She stepped in and I closed the door behind her. I helped her off with all the wool and was surprised to see how her face was healing. She wasn't pretty. She was beautiful.

"Come through to the kitchen. I was just making a steak. Are you hungry?"

She stopped. "Oh, God! I'm sorry, Harry. I should go and come back another time. I'm probably just being stupid."

"Come on." I went back, put an arm around her shoulder and guided her toward the kitchen. "Did you eat? Can you manage a steak to keep me company?"

"No. I mean yes, I could. No I haven't eaten. Thank you. But I don't want to intrude."

I pulled two cold beers from the fridge and showed them to her. She nodded and I pulled two cold glasses from the freezer. As I cracked them and poured I asked her, "So why are you scared?"

"A policeman came to see me. A Detective McDonald. He said he was investigating Johnny's death, and wanted to know if I knew him."

"What did you tell him?"

"Nothing. I said I hardly knew Johnny, that I'd eaten in his bar a couple of times. And anyway I didn't have time to talk to him right then. He didn't insist. He just went away." I handed her her beer and she took it. "But, Harry?"

"Yeah."

"He really scared me. There was something about him. He was cold, and creepy. Who is he?"

"I don't know," I said. "I don't know."

She took a small sip and I drained half my glass. As I set it down she said, "Can I stay here tonight?"

"Yeah," I said, and smiled. "Of course you can."

ELEVEN

I awoke at six. She was lying next to me, asleep. I rose, and as I shaved I held my eye in the mirror. My reflection told me it did not approve of what I had done. I told my reflection I didn't give a damn what it approved of.

I showered hot and cold, and went down to my gym where I worked out for a couple of hours before having a sauna and another cold shower. By the time I got up to the kitchen she was making coffee, barefoot in jeans, with a loose blouse. She gave me a shy smile.

"I didn't know where you were."

"I get up early. I was in the gym."

"You want me to make breakfast? I don't want to intrude and start messing up your daily routine."

"I have to go out. You help yourself to bread, eggs, bacon, ham." She nodded, looking down at the floor. I felt like a heel but ignored it. "I don't know how long I'll be. I want you to do me a favor."

"Sure, anything." She still wouldn't meet my eye.

"Stay put. Don't answer the phone. Don't open the door. Don't go out till I get back."

She listened to all this frowning at her feet. When I was done she asked, "Why?"

"I can't really explain now, Angel."

"Is it to do with Detective McDonald?"

"I'm not sure he is a detective. I have some friends looking into his background. I didn't want to involve you in all this, but it just kind of happened. I'm sorry."

She smiled. It was a sad kind of smile. "Not a very romantic morning after, huh?"

"I guess not. Let's get this little problem sorted, then we'll talk."

She was looking at her feet again. "Candlelit dinner talk, or 'Sit down, we need to talk,' talk?"

It was a good question, and I wasn't sure I knew the answer. I said, "You'll have to help me make that choice."

"OK."

"Stay put."

She nodded, I grabbed the attaché case I'd prepared the night before and I left.

It was a longer drive than you'd expect. I went via Randall's Island and the Robert F. Kennedy Bridge. I drove too fast, feeling impatient to get through Brooklyn and Queens, but once I'd passed Flushing Meadows I began to relax, and once I had left North Hills behind me, and the trees started to encroach on the Long Island Expressway, I eased my foot off the pedal and began to enjoy the ride.

I had kept one eye on my rearview mirror to see if McDonald was on my tail. I hadn't seen him so far, but then this guy was apparently so subtle he was practically invisible. The other possibility was that the brigadier might have interceded and got somebody to sit on McDonald—assuming he was a cop like he said he was.

One thing was for sure, whoever or whatever he was, McDonald knew an awful lot about a small aspect of my life. But he didn't have a clue about COBRA. And that fact might just save my skin.

It took me a little over two hours to reach Montauk, way out on the flat, narrow spit that reaches into the north Atlantic, like a pointing finger at the end of Long Island. I passed the town and kept going, beyond Fort Pond and into the dense woodlands, turning to russet and red in the early autumn, the time of mists and mellow fruitfulness, under a maturing sun.

I came at last to a fork in the road. There was a riding stables on my left and on my right a narrow road that plunged in among the trees. I slowed and took that narrow path. As I progressed the road became narrower and the forests either side became deeper and darker, and encroached further on the blacktop. There was room for only one car, and I wondered what would happen if I encountered someone coming the other way.

That didn't happen and eventually, at shortly before eleven AM, I came to a large wooden gate. Beside it there was a quaint sign that read "Hero's Cottage," and beyond it there was a drive through an unkempt lawn to a green garage door, where dappled shade made the grass a luminous green.

I climbed out of the TVR and pushed open the gate. The cottage was picture book, with two floors and an ancient gabled roof. The doors and windows had heavy wooden frames and I guessed it might have been as much as two or three hundred years old.

I drove in and closed the gate behind me, and followed the drive down to the garage that, on closer inspection, looked like it might have been added on to the house in the 1920s or '30s. It was faded redbrick with two big, wooden doors that had been painted military green long ago, and had started to peel. Inside, when I heaved open the doors, it smelled of creosote and musty shadows. I parked the car, grabbed the attaché case, closed the garage doors and let myself into the house.

There was a musty entrance hall with an old sage green carpet, a small hat stand with a mirror on the right, and a staircase with a white banister which climbed the right-hand wall into shadows. Between the hat stand and the staircase there was a white door which stood partially open onto a cottagey living room with a fireplace and big, floral armchairs.

On the left there was another door. This one was closed, but beyond the staircase I could see an open one and through it bright light, tinged with the green of a lawn and abundant trees. I could also see a sink and a pine table. I waited a moment, listening.

There was only silence.

I went into the living room. It was what you'd expect. A big floral sofa, two winged armchairs of the same design, an open fireplace with a basket of logs beside it. A couple of bookcases held paperbacks by Agatha Christie, Rex Stout, Le Carré and Raymond Chandler, and I wondered if this was evidence of the brigadier's hand.

French doors led out to a patio, and beyond the patio a long lawn bordered by cypress trees and pines. A small wooden gate at the far end gave access to a narrow path that led down to the beach. The ocean looked dark and cold.

I returned to the hall and opened the only door that had stood closed, across the hall from the living room. It was a dining room. It had a polished, oval table in the center and six chairs ranged around it. A doily in the middle held a silver candelabra. There was a threadbare Persian rug on the floor and prints on the walls showing fox hunting scenes. They might have been English or American. The dining room had two doors. One led to the hall, the other led to the kitchen.

It was in the kitchen that I found a shopping bag sitting on the large kitchen table. Inside there were four kilos—eight and a half pounds—of premium-grade raw opium. There was also a pound of C4 and a handful of remote detonators which I could configure to my cell. I broke up the cake and set the charges where I wanted them, taking care to visualize the scene as it would be.

When I was done I went back to the living room, sat in one of those comfortable floral armchairs and started reading the preliminary report the brigadier had sent me, on Alistair McDonald.

As he had told me already, the Bureau's New York field office had no record of a Special Agent Alistair McDonald. So they had looked into Gregorio McDonald to see if he'd had any children, and if so, who they were. As it turned out he'd had seven sons that they knew of, and two daughters. Two of the boys and none of the girls were legitimate. The two legitimate boys had been born to his wife, Olga Maria. The other seven kids were mainly with three prostitutes who'd worked in his clubs, but two were from the mistress he kept in town. None of them was called Alistair. They all had Mexican names: Armando, Eulogio, Nelson, Fermin, Ambrosio, Sancho and Francisco, all aged between twenty-two (Armando, studying marine biology at Columbia), and thirty-six (Francisco, practicing law in the Financial District of Manhattan). That left Ambrosio and Sancho who might fall within Alastair's probable age bracket. They also happened to be his only legitimate kids.

The girls were Maria, twenty-one and studying journalism at UCLA, and Carla, twenty-four, who had gone to Paris to study art. Who says crime doesn't pay?

There wasn't much else, but the two prime candidates were clearly not working for the NYPD. I went into the kitchen to make some coffee and stood staring out of the window at the long lawn, the small gate and the dark ocean. And all I could think of was that the whole thing was culturally wrong. I remembered McDonald well. He was brash, loud, aggressive. He was one of those Mexicans who could just as easily be Texan. He had all the aggression of the Scots and all the swagger of the Mexicans. Or was that the other way around: the swagger of the Scots and the aggression of the Mexicans?

I thought back to what had happened before I worked for COBRA. I had just left the SAS and returned to New York. I couldn't find a job and wound up working as a doorman at the Mescal Club. The boss, Mr. Rusanov, had told me one Gregorio

McDonald would be coming to cause trouble, and I was not to let him in.

The guy had eventually turned up in a red Ferrari, a cream suit and cowboy boots. Riding on his tail was a Chevy truck, and I just knew it was full of armed men. On his arm he had a stunning woman who had probably been made that morning out of silicon, Botox and AI chips. I remember noticing as he approached that he kept stroking his thin, pencil mustache. The woman clung to his arm with both of hers and gazed up at him.

When they'd arrived at the door I had blocked it with my body and asked him: "Are you Gregorio McDonald?"

The question had enraged him. He had flushed red and half-screamed at me, "I am Gregorio McDonald! Now get the fock..."

He'd had that odd trick a lot of Mexicans have, of making the U in "fuck" sound like the O in "dock." I'd told him he couldn't come in, and asked him to leave. I remembered telling him: "And tell your boys in the Chevy to get out of the parking lot."

He had answered, stabbing a finger at me in the air. "You get out of my *fockin'* way, gringo. I wanna see Peter. He's expectin' me and when I tell him..."

I hadn't let him get any further. "You have to leave."

I remembered he had gone crazy, screaming that he had to see Rusanov, that he had a business proposition for him and I had to let him in. I remembered my last words to him like it had been ten minutes earlier. I'd told him, "For the last time, Mr. McDonald. You have to leave."

I remembered his screaming face thrust into mine. He had crossed the red line and come too close. I smacked him in the jaw and he went down. I knew what would come next, so I ran for the Chevy. I had three or four seconds. Then the boys in the van would be spilling out shooting anything that moved.

I got there as the side-panel door slid open. There was a guy in denim with bare arms and an AK47. I acted without thinking. I grabbed the door and slammed it closed, practically guillotining his forearm. He had probably screamed, but I was focused on the

AK47 he'd dropped. I'd caught it before it hit the ground, shoved the barrel into the cab and let off a short burst. Then I'd shoved it through the sliding side door and emptied the magazine. It was probably about twenty-four rounds, but in an enclosed, metal box the ricochets made it more like a hundred and fifty.

I had wiped my prints and set it up to look like they had killed each other. Then I had returned to the door and told McDonald's girl to scram. She'd taken his car keys and his Ferrari and run, while I dragged McDonald inside by the scruff of his neck. I still remembered the look of terror on his face.

I remembered her face too, as she drove away. In spite of the terror she must have been feeling, it was rigid and expressionless because of the Botox. Like an android.

I had dragged him through the throbbing, flashing lights up the wooden stairs to where Rusanov was sitting with his boys and girls. There I had handed him over, knowing what they would do to him.

Now, I thought, looking at the still light glistening on the dark sea, they were all dead. All of them. And I had killed them all.

Except McDonald. He was the only one I had not killed. They had killed him later that night. They had cut off his head and his hands and dumped him by the bridge. And now somebody wanted me to pay for that.

I sat and drank my coffee, trying to fit all the pieces I could into a jigsaw puzzle that shifted and changed every time you added a new piece. But some kind of shape began to emerge. I began to realize who Alistair McDonald was, and with that realization I felt a sudden urgency to get back to Manhattan.

I inspected the house, satisfied myself nobody had been there but the delivery guy, and rolled the big TVR out of the garage. Then I started the long drive back to my house.

It was closing on three PM by the time I pulled in to James Baldwin Place from 5th Avenue. The first thing that struck me was that somebody had parked in my space, outside my house. I pulled in abruptly behind a Ford truck outside the apartment block at the intersection and killed the engine. I was maybe fifty yards away and, on the stoop, I could see Angel. She was leaning against one of the pillars with her arms crossed, and seemed to be talking. Three or four steps down from her was McDonald. They talked for about thirty seconds, then he climbed two steps so he was right up close to her, less than an arm's length. She didn't budge. Finally he turned, trotted down the steps, climbed into his Taurus and drove away.

Angel pushed herself off the pillar and disappeared into the porch. I counted fifteen to give her time to close the door, fired up the TVR and growled my way down the road to park in my space. There I sat and thought for a full five minutes before I climbed out, climbed up the stoop, and let myself in. As I closed the door Angel emerged from the kitchen, smiling.

"Hi!" I returned the smile. She hesitated a moment, then came over and gave me a kiss. After she'd done it she looked into my face, her eyes darting, searching my expression.

"Is that OK?"

"Of course." I cupped her face in my hands and she leaned her cheek into my palm. I sighed. "I'm sorry. I have a lot on my mind. I wish I could share it with you, but I can't. It will soon be over and then I promise to be less uptight."

"You want some coffee? Did you eat lunch?" I shook my head to both. She went up slightly on her toes. "Shall I make you some eggs?"

"That would be nice."

She hurried into the kitchen. I followed more slowly and leaned on the doorjamb while she looked for a frying pan.

"Any news or developments? Any phone calls?"

She was hunkered down pulling a bright orange cast-iron pan from a cupboard.

"Nobody phoned, but that Detective McDonald showed up about fifteen minutes ago, just before you arrived." She put the pan on the stove and went to the fridge, glancing at me as she went. "I wasn't going to open to him, like you said, but he called through the letter box and said he knew I was here, and he'd come back with four cars and a battering ram if I didn't open up. I didn't know if he could do that, so I thought I'd better be safe than sorry and I went out on the stoop and told him to go away."

I nodded. "You did the right thing."

"Can he do that? Knock the door down?"

I shook my head. "No. What did he ask you?"

"He wanted to know where you were."

"What did you tell him?"

"I said I didn't know where you were. I was still asleep when you went out. He said how come I was at your house? What was our relationship?" Her cheeks went bright red. "I didn't know what to tell him, but I wanted to make it as normal as possible, right? So I said I was your girlfriend. We'd met just a couple of days ago, but you'd been like this knight in shining armor for me, and we'd just fallen for each other." She shrugged. "I'm sorry if..." She trailed off.

I smiled. "Don't be sorry. Like I said, you did the right thing. We said we hadn't decided yet, remember?"

She nodded, still embarrassed. "Yeah."

TWELVE

I WENT UP TO MY STUDY WHILE SHE PREPARED LUNCH, and called Benini. Cleft Pallet handed me over to his boss with a, "Hey Boh, I'foyou." A second later his boss said, "Benini," like it was an answer to a question I hadn't asked.

"I have four kilos of pure, premium-grade product for you. That's eight and a half pounds. You want it?"

"Of course I want it."

"OK, tomorrow morning I'll send you an address. You come in one car. I see more than one car the deal is off and there will be consequences. I will be alone. You can bring your boys, but no more than four. You bring your laptop and you make the transfer so I can see it. When the money appears in Mr. Shir's account you get the product. Is that clear?"

"It's clear. But four kilos of product does not add up to the four million bucks I am paying over."

He'd slipped back again. I sighed. "Again? You are getting over a ton of product, Benini. And with the shit that's going down in Afghanistan you'd better get your hands on it fast, because prices are going to go through the roof when the Taliban start shooting all the farmers. Wise up!"

"OK, OK..." Like he'd heard it all before. "I'll be there."

I hung up and made my way back downstairs where Angel had set the table in the kitchen and was dishing up scrambled eggs and mushrooms. I pulled out a chair and sat.

"Looks good."

She didn't answer. She pulled out the chair opposite and said, "You sound like an automaton."

I glanced at her. She looked mad. She'd obviously been thinking while I was upstairs. A dim voice in my head told me she had expected more when I got home. Before I could say anything, she went on, "You keep saying we are going to talk. I'm beginning to feel like a damned fool, hanging around, locked in, waiting for you to have a moment to discuss how *I* feel. Because you," she waved her right hand at me, "apparently *don't* feel! And I *promised* myself I was not going to do this!"

"Stop."

She did and after a moment I sighed and laid down my knife and fork.

"I don't expect you to understand, Angel, but this is a lot more difficult for me than it seems."

"I don't want to force you into anything, Harry! It's just, what happened happened. I don't normally sleep with guys I have just met, but this was different and *then* you seemed to feel something. The normal thing would have been for us to talk, spend the day together, find out some more about each other. But the next morning you were like this hunk of ice. This *iceberg!* All your emotions seemed to have frozen. And you walked out and left me alone, ordering me to 'stay put.' Before you were a really nice guy, and afterwards you were this robot."

"I'm sorry."

"See? There you go again. All the feeling of pack ice, only harder to melt. All the warmth of a weekend in northern Greenland, in January."

"I get the idea."

She sighed and shook her head. "Ah, forget it. I don't want to try and convince you we have something. It felt good to me, but it obviously felt wrong to you. That's fine. At least we didn't have time to become attached." She gave a small, bitter laugh, stabbing her eggs with her fork. "But somehow I don't think that's much of a problem for you!"

"Are you done?"

"I'm sorry."

"First of all, let me put you straight about something. Becoming attached to people is a problem for me. More than you imagine. And most of the time, for their good, I can't allow it to happen."

Her eyes, which had been focused on her plate, now shot up to look at me.

"In the second place, I don't need convincing. It did not feel wrong to me. It felt good. It felt right. But *that* is a problem."

She frowned and her voice was almost shrill. "*Why, for God's sake?*" I drew breath to try and answer, but she didn't let me. "Is it your age? Hell, you're not that much older than me! What, fifteen years? You're in your thirties, I'm in my twenties. And the way you're made, you'll probably outlive me! Is it experience? You think I'm naïve? I'm not as naïve as I look! And with time and experience, I can learn. I tell you, what I have been through in the last couple of years, I am maturing fast! You think I would be unfaithful because of the age difference?" Tears had sprung into her eyes and she was talking fast. "Pal, believe me, I am the most loyal, faithful person you will *ever* meet in your life!"

I stood, went around the table, pulled her to her feet and put my arms around her. It didn't shut her up. She clung to me and kept talking.

"All I want, all I've wanted all this time, is someone like you, someone strong and kind, who will hold me and care about me. I am not interested in other men. I just want you, Harry. Ever since..."

She trailed off, buried her face in my chest and started to sob convulsively.

After a moment I picked her up and carried her into the living room, where I set her on the sofa and sat beside her. I handed her my handkerchief and she blew her nose and dabbed her eyes.

"I'm not ill, you know," she said and gave a small laugh. "You're cute, but I will survive!"

I took her hand. "It's not because you're younger, it's not because you're inexperienced. It's because I have a couple of things that are complicating my life in a big way right now."

"That's code for another woman."

I shook my head, said, "There is no other woman," and wondered if I was lying. "I can't talk to you about it. It's confidential."

"You're a spy."

"Not exactly, but I just told you I can't talk about it. Now listen to me. There is something I have to do..."

She burst out laughing, with her wet cheeks glistening. Then she blew her nose again and pushed up into a sitting position, putting distance between me and her. She spoke, drying her cheeks on the back of her wrists.

"Where I'm going, you can't go. What I have to do, you can't be any part of... How does it go? He says all that to her just before he packs her on a plane and sends her to another continent."

"Stop it, Angel."

She looked away at the window. "I'm sick of being alone."

"I know how you feel. Now will you please listen to me and stop flying off the handle? I am talking about work. There is a job I have to do tomorrow. Until then I have to stay focused. But when it's over..." I trailed off, not sure what to say, or how to finish that sentence.

"Are you serious?"

"Yeah, I think I am."

"I don't want to morally blackmail you into anything. I just... I guess I am a bit in shock with all this. It just kind of came out of left field and I'm still reeling."

"Yeah, well, just because I seem to have all the warmth of a weekend in northern Greenland—in January—don't run away with the idea that I'm feeling any different. This has kind of rocked my world too."

We were silent for a moment, staring at each other. Eventually she said, "I guess under that rock-hard exterior you are human after all."

"Something like that."

"You were in special forces, right?"

"The British SAS, for eight years."

"You must have killed men." I nodded. She frowned. "Do they haunt you?"

"Some of them." I hesitated. "Mostly, the ones that haunt me are the ones I didn't kill. The ones that were killed by others, and I could not save."

"I don't understand."

"The worst nightmare, the one that lives with me, that haunts me every night." I paused, looking down at the denim on her jeans pressed up against my leg. "We were in Helmand, in Afghanistan. There were four of us. Our job was to seek and destroy high-value targets. We had approached a small village called Al-Landy, in the afternoon, and we were going to wait till nightfall to move in because sometimes the villagers left food and water out for us.

"But this day, about five in the afternoon, a string of trucks rolled in, packed with Taliban." I paused, feeling I should not tell her, but somehow unable to stop the flow of words. "You get used to seeing atrocities. It never stops horrifying you, making you sick, but you get used to it. You learn to live with it. You have no choice. But this was something different. It went beyond anything any of us had ever seen before.

"Their leader, a man called ben-Amini, just seemed to go crazy, and his men went crazy with him. They raped, tortured and murdered the entire village. Not a single person was left alive. Not a single body was left unviolated."

Her voice was barely a whisper. "Why?"

I gave a laugh that was all bitterness and no humor. "Because the coffee shop owner had arranged a collection. It was like a small savings club, to buy a TV. On hot summer evenings they'd all sit out in the town square and watch it, set up on a table outside the coffee shop. At eleven o'clock he'd switch it off and they'd all go home to bed.

"But according to ben-Amini, this was contrary to Islam and an insult to Allah."

"TV is contrary to Islam? How can TV be an insult to Allah?"

"Because in Islam it is strictly forbidden to make images of people or animals. Only God can do that. Apparently it's OK to murder, decapitate and rape people, but not to make, or even watch, images of people."

"For watching *TV?*"

"There were children, little kids, crying, helpless, begging for mercy for their parents... There was one little girl, she couldn't have been more than four years old. I still see her eyes every time I close mine." I shook my head. "I don't want to remember, but they come back to me at night. Every night. The dead, the dying children, and those watching them die."

The room was very silent. She reached out and took my hand.

"We watched it all happen, and there was nothing we could do, except..." I stopped. It came to me then in a slow unfolding of realization. I had never known until that moment what had happened to me that day, and now I said it. "Except swear revenge, on him and all those who live in that darkness."

When she spoke she sounded afraid. "That darkness can suck you in, Harry. You can end up becoming like them. You become your enemy."

"It hasn't happened so far."

"Are you sure?"

I glanced at her sharply. "So far I haven't raped or murdered any children."

She blushed. "I'm sorry."

I sighed and squeezed her hand. "I know what you mean. And I do sometimes think of—" I stopped dead.

"Of what?"

"Of trying to put it all behind me."

"Do you work hunting down people like ben-Amini, Harry?"

I crushed the almost overwhelming urge to tell her the truth, and nodded, then shrugged. "Something like that."

She leaned forward and hugged me. She felt warm and supple. After a moment she whispered in my ear, with warm, moist breath, "Harry, take me upstairs."

———

THAT NIGHT, in the darkness of the small hours, I felt her hand on my shoulder, shaking me softly. I opened my eyes and looked at the clock. It said it was three thirty. I felt her warm, moist breath on my ear.

"I heard somebody moving downstairs."

I slipped out of bed, slid the Sig from under the mattress and moved silently across the room to the door. I pulled it open and stepped onto the landing. There was a noise, a soft ferreting sort of noise and it was coming from the next floor down, from my study.

I moved down, three steps at a time, and flattened myself against the wall beside my study door. It was closed, but I could see a thin strip of light at the bottom, and soft noises were coming from inside.

I opened the door and stepped inside. McDonald spun away from my filing cabinet, aiming a .22 revolver at my head. A .22. The same caliber that killed the two guys who were watching my house. A .22 will make a mess of your brain because it has enough energy to penetrate the skull, but not enough to exit, so it just ricochets inside and tears up your gray matter. And a revolver has the great advantage that it does not leave behind casings.

I pulled the trigger and blew it right out of his grip. He went pale, bent double and clutched his hand between his legs. I noticed the window was open and wondered if the neighbors had heard the shot. In the bedroom above, I heard a thud. Then Angel's feet pounding down the stairs. A moment later she burst into the study.

I said, "Go back upstairs and stay there."

"Detective *McDonald?*"

He looked up and stared at her. He had tears in his eyes. Getting a gun shot out of your hand is extremely painful. I figured he had a couple of broken bones in his wrist. I said, "Angel, go upstairs and stay there."

"But—"

"Go! You are a liability here."

She turned and I heard her trot up the stairs. To McDonald I said, "What the hell do you think you're doing?" He didn't answer. I went on. "Any cop knows evidence obtained by theft will be ruled inadmissible in court. But what the hell were you hoping to find anyway?"

He rasped, "You murdered Gregorio McDonald! Or you were at least complicit in his murder."

I pushed the door closed, laid the Sig on my desk and approached him. "What makes that so important to you?"

"I'm a cop. We're supposed to nail bastards like you."

"Today you're a cop. Yesterday you were a federal agent. What will you be tomorrow, assuming this homicidal maniac allows you to leave alive?"

"You wouldn't. I could be wearing a wire."

"I know damn well you're not wearing a wire. I also know damn well you're not a cop. What's your story, McDonald? What are you looking for?"

"I told you, evidence you killed Gregorio McDonald."

I smiled and jerked my head at the cabinet. "And you think you'd find it in there?" He swallowed hard. I pointed at him. "Listen to me, I killed several men that night. I don't know how many. But I killed them all in self-defense. And there was no shortage of detectives at the 40th who would have liked to discuss the whole affair with me in detail. But they couldn't. You know why?" He didn't answer. He just stared at me, nursing his wrist and his hand. "I'll tell you why. Because they all knew, beyond a shadow of a doubt, that those boys had been killed by a professional, and there was not a shred of evidence on the face of the planet that could connect me with those hoods."

I paused. He was breathing heavily and the blood was draining from his face as shock began to kick in. I went on talking, very deliberately.

"But there was one person I did not kill that night, and that was Gregorio McDonald. I killed his boys, his date ran off in his Ferrari and I took him inside. Then my boss, Peter Rusanov, sent me home. My guess is that Peter Rusanov and his boys killed McDonald. Now, how about you tell me the truth before I start to lose my patience. What makes you so interested in Gregorio McDonald? And what's with the name? Same surname, but all his sons had Mexican names. Yours is Scottish. What the hell are you playing at?"

I heard the door open softly behind me and felt a stab of anger in my gut. I saw McDonald's eyes flick over my shoulder.

"Angel, please go upstairs! I do not need you here right now!"

Her voice came sobbing. "I can't leave you alone. And I am too *scared* to be alone. I don't know what's happening. I don't believe this man is a cop. What is he doing? Why is he persecuting?"

I felt her hand on my shoulder and turned. Her face was wet with tears. I started to say, "I'm going to call the cops..." when I saw her face disfigured with terror. I pushed her hard, heard the loud explosion of the Sig and felt the hot whisper of the round as it brushed my face. I turned and saw him waving the weapon wildly at me. I lunged for him and the cannon exploded again.

THIRTEEN

It exploded in his left hand at the very moment I ducked my head to my right and smacked the weapon away. I heard the round smack into the wall behind me, and Angel's voice cry out.

The desk was between us and he was moving about, waving my Sig in my face, trying to aim with his left hand. He had started screaming at me, *"Confess! Confess!"*

I put my hands up and took a step to my left, forcing him to turn with me. In my peripheral vision I could see the .22 on the floor. The round from my Sig had hit it a glancing blow, but the chances of it still working were slim. Worse, it could blow up in my hands. I said:

"I already told you everything. What the hell is the matter with you? You've become obsessed, McDonald. You need help. I can arrange that for you."

He gave a crazy, bitter laugh. "Oh, I bet you can! Sectioned in some private hospital in the Catskills, where I will never be seen again!"

"Get real, McDonald! Enough with the paranoid fantasies! I was a doorman! I handed him over to Rusanov..."

His voice was a shrill scream. *"You sentenced him to torture and death!"*

I roared, *"And what's it to you?"*

His eyes were bulging, staring. I was at the edge of the desk. The .22 was by my foot.

His neck went rigid, corded with bulging tendons. His face flushed red. He clenched his teeth like he was biting down on words he didn't want to say. I stepped forward, thrusting my face at the cannon, and roared, *"Come on!"* Then I leaned to my right, smacked my right hand into the barrel of the Sig and gripped it hard. It exploded for a third time and I heard a scurry and a whimper behind me. McDonald was making inarticulate noises and kicking at my shins with his foot. I ignored the pain and levered the pistol back toward his chest.

He knew what was coming next because he screamed, let go of the gun and fell across the desk. I swung round, trying to get a bead on him. To my right I saw Angel, with the .22 in her hands, aiming at him too. I snapped, "No! Hold your fire!" McDonald scrambled to his feet and staggered out the door, pounding down the stairs.

My instinct was to go after him, but I stopped myself and turned to Angel. She was trembling and crying. She set the revolver down on my desk like it was poisonous and stared into my face with horrified eyes.

"I almost shot him."

I set down the Sig. Downstairs I heard the front door slam and through the window I watched his shadowy figure running fast toward 5th Avenue. I turned back to Angel and picked up the revolver.

It was a beautiful thing: a Smith and Wesson Model 17 Masterpiece, built on Smith and Wesson's K-Frame, with blued steel and a wooden grip. The gun had adjustable sights and the action was like silk. Above all it was an extremely accurate weapon. With this kind of quality, and a price tag that came in at a thousand bucks, this was a connoisseur's gun. Most enthusiasts would turn their nose up at any kind of .22, and wouldn't dream of paying a grand for one. But this baby was worth every dollar. I examined it carefully, wondering what kind of man takes something like this along to burgle a house in search of evidence he must know he won't find.

My round had hit the rear sight and dented it. I spun the cylinder and listened. It sounded OK.

"You have been lucky," I said.

"Lucky?"

"When I shot it out of his hand, he must have moved. The round only hit it a glancing blow on the rear sight. If the impact had been a little lower down, it would have damaged the cylinder or the barrel, and the cartridge could have exploded in the gun when you pulled the trigger."

"Oh, I was trying to help you."

"I know."

"He got away."

I put my arm around her. "Don't worry. He won't go far."

"How did he get in?"

"That's what I'm wondering." I closed the window and secured it. "One thing is for sure, he did not scale the wall and come in through the window, much as he'd like us to think he did."

"He didn't?"

"No. Stay here a moment. I need to check something upstairs."

She reached for me. "Don't leave me alone, Harry."

"Two seconds. He's gone and I'll be right back. Just stay here."

I sprinted up to the attic. The dead bolt was in place, as I had expected, but on the step below it I found a small strip of black plastic. I put it in my pocket and went down to Angel, who was hugging her arms.

"You want to make us some coffee, and lace it with some scotch? I have to make a call."

"Please don't leave me alone!"

"Don't worry. I'll be right there beside you."

I pulled on some jeans and a shirt and we went down, and while she brewed the coffee I sat at the kitchen table and called the brigadier. He sounded sleepy.

"Are you going to call me every three hours, Harry? What is it this time?"

"We just had a visitor."

I heard him sit up and sigh. "We?"

"Angel stayed the night."

"That was stupid of you, Harry."

"As it turns out, it wasn't. I just told you we had a visitor."

"Who?"

"Alistair McDonald. He was in my study, trying to open my file cabinet."

"What have you got in there?"

"Six bottles of the Macallan."

"Perhaps he was thirsty."

It was a rare joke and it deserved a smile. I let one tinge my voice when I replied. "I keep the contents top secret. He said he was looking for proof I killed Gregorio McDonald at the Mescal Club."

I could almost hear him frown through the silence. "What the hell did he expect to find in your filing cabinet, an invoice?"

"Exactly."

"You think he had a different motive?"

"I have a hunch. He got awful hysterical. He seemed obsessed with finding that proof."

"Where is he now? Did you neutralize him?"

"Not exactly, no. But I have another question. What's with the corporal and the blades in the van? How did this guy get in? I thought we had eyes watching the place."

"I'll have a word with him."

"Actually, have the corporal come to the stoop. I have something McDonald left behind. It will have his prints on it. We should run them through AFIS."

"All right." He was about to hang up but hesitated. "Harry, is this girl clouding your judgment?"

"No. I think she's at risk and the safest place for her right now is here."

He sighed, unconvinced. "Very well."

I hung up and turned to Angel. She was pouring two cups of coffee.

"I'll be two minutes. Stay here and stay put. Understood?"

She nodded and I left the kitchen, crossed the hall and let myself out into the night, closing the door behind me. I sat on the top step and waited. A minute later a tall guy in jeans with a leather biker's jacket strolled up with his hands in his jacket pockets, and joined me on the stoop.

He said, "All right?" like we'd known each other all our lives.

"Yeah, you OK?" I didn't wait for an answer. I had the .22 in a transparent plastic bag. I handed it to him. He took it and turned it over a few times.

"Sweet. Accurate buggers. Not cheap." He looked up at me. "An aficionado's gun."

"Yeah. My thoughts too. Our visitor left it behind. I need it printed and tested for DNA in the next two or three hours."

He nodded and anticipated my next question. "We're on shifts, two and two. We didn't see anyone come in. He must be coming in from the back, up on the roof. And in case you're wondering. We saw the bloke leave at a run and asked permission to go after him. It was denied."

"How come you weren't sent to the house to investigate?"

"I was. I saw you at the window with the bird, saw you were OK and went back to the van. Last thing we want is a lot of people running up and down drawing attention to themselves." He shrugged. "I thought if you were well enough to walk you were well enough to call in help if you needed it."

"Fair enough. You'll get this to the lab for me?"

"No problem. You OK?"

I smiled. "Yeah. But I think our friend has a broken wrist."

He nodded. "He needs a good talking-to."

"Yeah." I nodded. "You're not wrong." We stood. "I don't think he'll be back, but all the same, maybe redeploy to 129th. Have a look around. See if you can find how he's getting in."

"Sure. Will do."

He sauntered down the steps and walked slowly across the road, back toward the van, like he had all the time in the world. Brits; anyone who thought they were all bumbling bowler hats and brollies was out of their minds.

I went back inside and found Angel looking pale and anxious in the kitchen.

"Is everything OK?"

I sat next to her and sipped the pungent coffee laced with scotch. It was good and welcome. As I set down the cup I said, "Everything's fine. I hope to have identified this guy by morning. I have to attend to something else before lunch, but in the early afternoon I'll go find him. Then we can put this whole, crazy business to rest once and for all."

She pulled her chair closer and rested her head on my shoulder, hugging my arm.

"Oh, hunny, I do hope so. Do you think..." She looked up at me as I took another sip. "Do you think we might... I'm afraid to say it, Harry."

"I think we might, Angel. But let's get tonight and tomorrow over with first. Then maybe we can go away for a week or two, somewhere peaceful, where we can think and talk in peace."

"Oh, Harry, that would be heaven!"

"Come on." I put my arm around her. "Let's get some sleep. I have a very early start tomorrow."

We stood and she stared up into my face, frowning, worried. "Who were you talking to on the phone, and," she glanced toward the door, "and outside?"

"It's best you don't know, Angel. But I have some guys,

friends, they were watching the wrong place. He was coming in through the back somehow, and up on the roof. They're watching the back now."

"Oh."

"They're good. They're professionals. But I doubt he's coming back anyway."

And we climbed the stairs up to the bedroom again, arm in arm.

A little later, as she drifted off to sleep, she whispered, "This has been awful, Harry, but I feel so close to you now, and so safe."

———

I GOT UP AT SEVEN, had a quick shower and a pot of strong, black coffee. I found the keys to the Land Rover on the mat and stepped out onto the stoop. It had rained during the night and the blacktop was wet, touched with reflected streetlight. The Land Rover was parked just behind the TVR. I climbed in and, just as the sun was starting to bleed through broken clouds on the eastern horizon, I set off for Montauk. I drove as fast as I could, staying within the speed limit. The last thing I needed was to get pulled over by the cops now. But at a time when everybody was headed into Manhattan, the roads out to the suburbs were relatively free of traffic, and I was able to make good progress. And as I drove I rehearsed everything I had to do.

I was pretty sure I had finally understood what was happening with McDonald, and that was something I told myself I would have to deal with when the Benini job was finished. I was also pretty sure it would keep till then. But as I drove certain things kept creeping into my thoughts again and again. His fervor, his near hysteria, his passion for a man who had never been his father, whom he had probably never met.

I remembered the brigadier's words: Who Dares Wins. It was our motto in the Regiment. Where fear and self-doubt can rob a man of all his skill, daring and courage can lend you skills and brilliance you never knew you had. Had that been the case with McDonald? If so, what was it that had given him that courage and daring in the first place? What was his beef with me? What was the source of his obsession with Gregorio McDonald?

And then there was the coincidence of the name. The Bard had asked, "What's in a name?" Nine times out of ten, there is nothing in a name. But in this case it was *all* about the name. The name was everything.

I shoved the thoughts firmly to the back of my mind and focused once again on the plan in hand. The routine I had to follow.

When I reached Flushing Meadows the gaps in the clouds had closed again and it had started to drizzle. I called Benini and gave him instruction on how to find the cottage. He said he'd be there in a couple of hours. I told him to make it two and a half and hung up. At eleven AM I pulled into the drive. I left the car facing the gate and crossed the wet lawn to the house. Inside, I double-checked everything I had prepared the day before.

Everything was in order, so I cleaned my Sig and sharpened the Fairbairn and Sykes, and settled down to wait.

At shortly before twelve noon I heard the rumble of an engine out front. I watched through the window as a man in an Italian suit, hunching his shoulders against the drizzle, pushed open the gate, and a moment later a dark blue Audi eased through and parked beside the Land Rover. Then two doors opened and two guys got out, one of them the driver. The other was my old friend, Tony. He opened an umbrella and the door for Benini, and then all four of them came to the front door. I opened it before they rang. Benini was scowling.

"You couldn't find anything more remote?"

"Yeah, next time we'll go to Wales, or Alaska. I hear it's nice in August."

"Smart-ass."

"Come in and quit griping, Benini. Every time I see you

you're complaining about something. It's bad for the troops' moral."

They came in and he scowled at me some more. "And you? Your mouth is always full of fuckin' words. Always with the smart answer."

"Yeah, I can afford that luxury. Kindly go through to the dining room."

They filed through and stood looking around. I said:

"You want to scan the room for bugs, cameras, anything else?"

He jerked his head at Tony and he and a big guy in his forties pulled out a couple of hand-held scanners and started going over the room. I gestured Benini to a chair at the table and we sat. I leaned my elbows on the table.

"I am going to show you a kilo of pure opium. Open it, test it, get one of your boys to smoke it if you like. You will not find better opium on the face of the planet. When you have tested the quality, you make the transfer, four million bucks, to the account I give you in Belize. Then I give you three more kilos of the same grade opium. Again, you are free to test it." I could see by his scowl he wasn't happy. I smiled on the right side of my face. "If you're not happy with the other three kilos, you can see I am alone and I am not wearing a wire. So you can start cutting bits off of me until I return the money. But I don't think you're going to want to do that. Not when you see the product."

A voice behind me said, "The room's clear, Boss."

Benini narrowed his eyes at me and his scowl slowly turned to a thin, unpleasant smile.

"I may well do that," he said. "Now show me this shit, and you had better not be wasting my time."

I left the room and went upstairs to get the first packet of pure brown sludge.

FOURTEEN

When I got back they had distributed themselves about the room more or less as I had expected. Benini was sitting at the dining table, where I had put him, like he was sitting at a large desk. Tony was standing by the door with his hands clasped in front of his balls, like Adam before he found the leaf, and one knee giving an occasional jerk.

The big, older guy was behind Benini, on his right, in the same position, only he'd lost the youthful jerk of the knee over the years. The third guy was the chauffer. He was behind Benini on his left. Same pose. They'd seen it on TV so I guess it was mandatory.

I dumped the plastic pack of dope on the table. It made a heavy thud and all eyes gravitated to it. I sat.

"Test it. Premium Afghan poppy resin. You won't find purer, better opium on the market."

He sat nodding at it. His face was becoming more rigid by the second.

"Let me tell you," he said at last, without looking at me, "let me tell you what is making me mad about this whole thing. You keep talking that talk, and you keep convincing me. But then you go away and I think about it and I start getting mad again."

I saw the big guy and the chauffeur straighten and look at me. They'd caught the tone in Benini's voice, like I had, and they knew there was a ninety percent chance they were going to have to kill me.

Benini's eyes traveled up from the table to meet mine.

"This," he picked up the cake of dope, looked at it and looked at me, "this is costing me *one million dollars?* Do I *look* stupid? What are you saying? You saying I look like a dumb fuck?"

I leaned back in my chair. My heart was pounding, but that was between me and my heart. Today was as good a day to die as any. I may as well go down looking cool.

"You came all the way out to Montauk to ask me that? Well, Benini, I gotta tell you, right now the answer is yes. You look like a dumb fuck. You're wasting your time, my time, and what's worse, you're wasting Mr. Fateh Shir's time. Why didn't you tell me this..."

He smashed his fist on the table and screamed at me. "*I don't give a damn about your fuckin' Fatty Shit!*" Total silence fell on the room. "*I am the power here!*" He pounded his chest with his open hand. "This is New York, not fuckin' Afghanistan! *Nobody* threatens me in New York!"

His ego had made its point and my face was making the point back that it wasn't all that impressed.

"You done?"

"No!" He pointed at me, with his elbow on the table. "You want to know why I didn't tell you this yesterday?"

"I was wondering."

"Because my anger has been building hour by hour. Because you and your Fatty Shit don't treat me with respect! And in New York I *demand* respect!"

I gave a reluctant nod and sighed.

"Fine, *Mr.* Benini, I *respectfully* request that you allow me to explain why you are not paying a million dollars for one pound of premium Afghan opium. Will you allow me to do that?"

The boys relaxed. Greed and suspicion crept jointly onto Benini's face, but the homicidal mania retreated. He sat back.

"OK," he said, "convince me."

I pointed at the packet. "Each of these is a kilo. That's a little over thirty-five ounces."

"So I am paying a million bucks for thirty-five ounces."

"If you want me to explain you are going to have to let me talk, and you're going to have to listen."

He didn't say anything so I went on. "You are actually getting four kilos of pure, premium-grade opium. And that is part one of the points I am making to you. Because you are not going to sell four kilos of premium opium. You are going to break it down to thirty, or even twenty, percent purity before you even start thinking about selling it or processing it as heroin. That means that each one of these cakes will become three cakes. That's between twelve thousand and twenty thousand grams. Retailing at about forty to fifty bucks a gram, you could be making between one and two hundred and fifty thousand bucks per cake, at *current* prices."

He was still scowling. He drew breath and I interrupted him.

"Times four. That's a potential return of one million dollars on these four cakes, without converting one ounce into heroin." I sat forward and pointed at him. "But before you start griping about that being one quarter of what I am asking you to spend, let me remind you of two things. One." I held up an index finger. "With the withdrawal of US troops from Afghanistan, the Taliban are closing down all the opium farms. Mr. Shir, because he has close ties with the Taliban, will be one of the few who are allowed to continue growing and shipping. What does that mean? It means that the price of opium is going to go through the roof!" I pointed at the ceiling, in case he didn't know where the roof was. "So your *actual* return on these four cakes could be double what I am saying or more. Opium, Mr. Benini, is *highly* addictive, and this will be a seller's market."

I held up two fingers. "Second, what I don't seem to have

made you understand is that these four cakes are a gesture of goodwill, to persuade you of the quality of our product—and that we mean business. So on receipt of your payment we will ship to you *one hundred kilos* of pure, premium, Afghan opium. Not ninety-six kilos. One hundred kilos. These are a gift. What you are paying for does not include these four cakes."

He grunted. "It's still four million bucks."

I gave a single, dry bark of a laugh. "You will make well over twenty million on your first shipment. And these four cakes will be a small bonus on top. The next eleven shipments will be pure, net profit."

He thought about it for a full minute. You got the feeling it wasn't so much that he didn't trust me and Fateh Shir, but the pain of handing over four million bucks in one go was too much to bear. In the end I sighed and made to stand.

"I'm sorry, Mr. Benini. I made a mistake. I told Mr. Shir that you were the man for this operation because you were a tough, old-school risk taker with a network that could take care of things." I shrugged. "Time takes its toll, I guess, and we grow tired of taking risks..."

His face flushed. "Just one goddamn minute. A man needs time to think before making a decision like this! Tony! My case!"

Tony turned and left the room. I heard the front door open and close and figured he was going to the car. I kept watching Benini with an expression on my face that said I was lingering somewhere between disappointment and contempt, and was still sitting there through mere courtesy.

A moment later the door opened again and Tony entered with an attaché case. He set it on the table in front of Benini. Benini entered a code, flipped the catches and opened what turned out to be a laptop computer. He rattled at it for a minute, then spun it so I could see the screen. It was the transfers page of a well-known international bank favored by those wishing to launder their money. There was a dialogue box open with a winking cursor in it.

"Your account number," he said.

I typed it in and turned it back to him. He did some more typing and hit the enter key. Then he scowled at me like a man who has just had his balls amputated. "If this is a scam, Mr. Smith, I will not rest until I have found you and..."

"Stop there, Mr. Benini, before you say something we might both regret. Let's start this enterprise on a cordial footing."

I heard a ping on my phone and checked the screen. It was the confirmation that four million bucks had been deposited in my account in Belize. The spoils of war. I smiled.

"Thank you, Mr. Benini. Mr. Shir will be very happy, and I promise you he can be a very generous friend. Let me go and get the remaining cakes of resin, and then perhaps you will toast the future of this project with me. I have an exceptionally good twenty-five-year-old Macallan."

He nodded and I went upstairs to get the remaining packages of dope. When I got back down I placed my own attaché case on the table and opened it for him to see. He nodded. I said:

"You brought some digital scales?"

Again he jerked his head at Tony. Tony turned to the big guy. "GG, you got the scales?"

"I thought you had'm."

"No, I *told* you when we got outta the car, bring the scales."

"No, you said I *got* the scales."

I sighed and raised an eyebrow at Benini, who roared, *"Angelo! Go get the fuckin' scales from the fuckin' car!"*

The chauffeur who was standing behind his left shoulder left the room while Tony and GG did a lot of shrugging.

"Sorry, Boss."

"I thought he said he had 'em."

Benini ignored them both and picked up the first pack I'd given him. "Tony, you got a knife, or did you forget to bring that too?"

"No, I got a knife."

He pulled a switchblade from his pocket, clicked it open and handed it to his boss. Benini took it and gave me a meaningful look. He now did what he should have done before transferring the money. He slipped the blade into the package and pulled the blade out caked with a sticky, toffee-like substance. He smelled it and put a tiny amount on the end of his tongue. He glanced at me.

"The rest is like this?"

The door opened and Angelo came back in with the scales. I said, "Of course it is. Try the other cakes."

Angelo set the scales down in front of him and he methodically weighed each cake. He nodded after each one and said, "Each one is a couple of grams over a kilo. You have been true to your word. The quality of the first cake is everything you said it was."

He took another pack and pierced it, smelled it and tasted it on his tongue. He handed the blade to GG, who also tested it and handed it back. Benini repeated the operation on the third package and then set the fourth one in front of him and smiled.

"But you know what? I still feel like I am paying four million bucks for four kilos of opium. And I don't like that feeling. So, here's the thing. I gotta be grateful to you, Mr. Smith, because you gave me an idea. It was a good idea. I am going to keep this generous gift from Fatty Shit, but he can take his ton of dope and stick it up his ass. I don't want it. And I am going to ask you to return my money to me. Now."

I smiled. I even chuckled a little. "I can't do that, Mr. Benini."

"Remember what you said to me? That we could start removing bits of you until you transferred the money back? Well, that was what I thought was an excellent idea. And you know the one thing Tony did not forget in the car?"

Tony piped up, "It was GG."

"He did not forget the pliers. I think we'll start with the toes, and then see where the fancy takes us."

I raised a finger and held up the phone. I spoke as I stood and took a step back. "No need for that, gentlemen. I can't guarantee how Mr. Shir will respond, but if you are *that* unhappy with the operation, I will most certainly return your money. No need for bloodshed."

I pressed nine on my keypad and the three ounces of C4 that were sitting in the cake in front of Benini exploded. Simultaneously the three cakes I'd put behind the hunting prints where GG, Tony and Angelo were standing exploded too. I didn't stop to see what damage they had done. I pulled the Sig from under my arm, hunkered down and turned toward Tony all in one movement.

Tony had reacted by dropping to the floor. Swearing profusely, he rolled and I tried to get a bead on him. Next thing he had his piece in his hand and was waving it in my direction. I dived behind the desk, heard a slug tear into the floor and the dining-room door open. Then there was Tony's feet running for the front door.

I stood and looked down at Benini. He was in bad shape, groaning, with his eyes rolling back in his head. I shot him through the temple and finished off GG and Angelo too. I reached in Angelo's pocket and found the key to Benini's car. Then I went after Tony.

By the time I got to the door he was clambering into the driver's seat of the Audi. He slammed the door and I heard a violent oath as he realized he didn't have the keys. I figured the windows and the chassis were bulletproof, and as I thought that, I heard the locks engage. He could close the doors because I was close enough with the key. But he could not start the engine with the key on the outside. I walked to the rain-spattered windshield and smiled at him. I held up the last four ounces of C4 for him to see. It's a habit I have, to always hold a little back.

His face said four ounces of C4 was not going to scratch the paint on his boss's car. I nodded and walked slowly round to the gas cap, with the rain beginning to trickle down my neck. I opened the cap and held up the C4 for him to see it in the wing mirror. I heard a muffled scream from inside the car, the door was flung open and Tony half fell out, slipping in the muddy grass, holding up his hands.

"OK! OK! I give up. I give up, man! I'll do anything! Just tell me what you want!"

I double tapped and put two 9mm slugs through his skull.

I went over to confirm the kill and told him, "You asked. That was what I wanted, Tony."

I dragged him into the garage, went back inside the cottage, collected Benini's laptop and the contents of his pockets, dropped the key to the Audi on Angelo's belly and made my way out to the Land Rover. There I fired up the engine and pulled out of the gate. When I was moving down the track I called the brigadier.

"Report."

"The job is done. I only made very small explosions, but you need a cleanup team in pretty short order. The place is a mess and there is an Audi in the front yard."

"Good, well done. What are you going to do now?"

"I'm going to go and look for Alistair McDonald."

FIFTEEN

The brigadier put me up to speed on what they had gathered from his prints and the DNA on the pistol. It was pretty much what I had expected. He also told me his real name was Brad Hoight and, as I had begun to suspect, he was a private investigator working out of an office at 250 Brook Avenue, in Mott Haven. His apartment was at 576, 139th Street, a block from his office. He had some form, but not much. Mainly petty theft, low-level extortion, blackmail running into hundreds rather than thousands of dollars, and acts of violence when drunk, mainly against prostitutes—and which wound up hurting him more than he hurt them. His last such outburst having put him in hospital for a month with a broken leg and internal hemorrhaging.

It also turned out that the Smith and Wesson .22 had been registered to Gregorio McDonald, along with thirty-six other weapons. That didn't surprise me. It was exactly the kind of gun Gregorio would have had in his collection. Neither did it surprise me that the weapon had not been reregistered since his death.

I sighed to myself as I pulled onto the Old Montauk Highway and headed west. Whatever I ended up doing with McDonald AKA Brad Hoight, first I was going to have a long conversation with him.

By the time I got to Mott Haven it was five thirty in the afternoon. The heavy clouds were forcing a premature dusk, and lights were starting to come on. I parked outside a fast-food shop on the corner and crossed the road to an elaborate, crimson-arched doorway with a dull, mat-gray door set into it. There were small plastic bells by the door and Three B had a faded card in it that read, "Hoight PI."

I rang it and nothing happened. I rang again three times and three times the same nothing happened, so I pulled out my Swiss Army Knife, shoved it in the lock, gave it a smack and opened the door.

The stairs were narrow, wooden and paint stained, partially covered in a threadbare carpet of unknown color. The light was not a bare bulb, but it may as well have been. The shades were fly-blown green Bakelite, shaped like 1950s flying saucers.

I climbed to the third floor and found apartment B. It had a plaque on the door that read, HOIGHT PRIVATE INVESTI-GATOR. I knocked and nothing happened except that a door down the hall opened and a TV got louder. I looked and scowled, and snarled, "Who told you you could leave your TV? Get back to your programming at once!"

I chuckled as the door slammed and feet scurried back to the hive interface. I gave the door the same Swiss Army treatment and it eased open.

The block had probably been built in the early 1900s and by the looks of it not much had been done to it since then. There was a dull light in a globe in the center of the ceiling, a desk up against the far wall which showed no signs of being used, a couple of straight-backed chairs and another door opposite. I closed the one I had just opened and crossed the floor. The second door was not locked. The room it gave access to was about fifteen foot square, carpeted in faded blue and furnished with a wooden desk that looked like it had been rescued from a junkyard. There were also two green, steel filing cabinets, and a couple of bentwood chairs that sat on the client's side of the desk.

I rummaged through the drawers in the desk and found paper clips. I jimmied the filing cabinets and found somewhere in the region of two hundred surveillance cases. About ninety percent were men who wanted to know if their wives were cheating on them. Apparently about ninety percent of them were. The other ten percent were women who wanted to know if their husbands were cheating on them. The same percentages held.

The only thing of interest was the fact that his last documented case had been two months earlier, and if the dust on the furniture and the fungus on the piece of pizza in his wastepaper basket were anything to go by, that was about the last time he was in the office.

I wiped my prints, left the office and made my way down to the Land Rover again. I climbed into the cab and rolled around to 139th with the wipers squeaking like they were bored and wanted to go home already.

He lived in a big, yellow-brick apartment block with crumbling stucco on the arch of the door and on the window frames. The door, which was made of ugly, chromed steel bars, was open. A short passage led to a small lobby and an ancient elevator with graffiti praising the intimate prowess of certain ladies.

I climbed the stairs to the fifth floor and found Door C. I rang the bell and once again got no reply. Two more rings got the same answer. So I once again picked the lock and went in, closing the door quietly behind me.

I was in a short passage carpeted in what had once been beige before giving up hope. On the right, an open doorway gave on to a small kitchenette where, instead of a left-hand wall, there was a kind of breakfast bar. The only things on it were a stained coffee cup and an ashtray full of butts. Camel. In the sink there were five dirty plates, mostly with the remains of eggs and bacon and fast-food burgers. There were also two mugs and two glasses. The glasses smelled of tequila. One of the cups had black coffee residue, the other had white. So he had recently had a visitor. In the trash were the Styrofoam boxes in which the burgers had arrived. I also saw an empty bottle of tequila. The Continental Op would have been proud of me.

On the work surface there was a two-ring cooker. Sitting on it was a frying pan with evidence of having been used multiple times without having been washed. In the fridge there were one and a half six-packs of beer and a couple of packs of burgers which were out of date. It seemed he hadn't been shopping for a while. At least not for food. It was all slightly at odds with the athletic, well-dressed man I had seen, and I wondered if, like his scuffed shoes and his tired suit, it was all evidence of a man in decline.

I made my way around the breakfast bar and into the living room. There was an IKEA coffee table in the middle of the floor. There were also an IKEA sofa and armchair which were probably new when Margaret I established the Kalmar Union.

There was a flat-screen TV on a melamine dresser, and beside it there was a photograph in a frame of a ten year-old Hoight standing in a park next to a couple who might have been his mother and father. He was holding the man's hand. Nobody was smiling. It struck me the dresser and the coffee table were remark-ably clean compared to the kitchen and the TV screen.

The bedroom was illuminated by a window which overlooked 139th Street and the East Bronx Early Childhood Center. The blind was up, showing a wet street with desultory, sighing cars. The bed was a torrid tangle of sheets, slightly grayed from too much use and perspiration, and not enough washing.

The freestanding wardrobe held a couple of suits, shirts, pants: what you'd expect. It was the same story with the chest of drawers: shorts, socks, sweaters, sheets and pillowcases.

There were bedside tables either side of the bed. Each held a lamp and each was uncharacteristically clean. I hunkered down on the right side of the bed, beside the wardrobe, and breathed heavily on the imitation pine surface of the table. For a few seconds you could just make out the ring of a glass.

I moved to the other side of the bed and performed the same test. I got the same result. So either Hoight slept on the right side of the bed on even days, and on the left on odd days, or he had recently shared his bed with someone who took milk in her coffee and didn't want anyone to know she'd been here. Or he didn't want it known. Either or both.

But—I stood and thought—that didn't make much sense. Why go to the trouble of cleaning the bedside tables and the dresser, but leave the cup in the sink and the cigarettes in the ashtray?

The drawer in the bedside table revealed little but the smell of gun oil, a magazine for a Glock 19 and the logical deduction that Hoight slept on that side of the bed. There was also a box of 9mm cartridges; not .22s, 9mms. I thought about that and decided it made sense.

In the bedside table on his sleeping partner's side, I found a pack of Camels, a blue disposable lighter and a pair of long, dangly earrings. I left them where they were and went back to the kitchen.

Sometimes you get lucky. Most times you don't get lucky, you just reap the rewards from being thorough and paying attention. I was about to give up and return to the car when I noticed the trash can. It was half full, which meant that most of the trash in it would be relatively recent. I found a refuse sack in one of the kitchen drawers, split the two side seams and spread it out on the surface beside the sink. Then I dumped the trash on it, set the can beside it and started methodically working through the trash and putting it back in the can. There was nothing in the way of peel and very little in the way of organic matter. Most of it was fast-food containers and half-empty sachets of ketchup, mixed in with half-crushed beer cans. There was also cigarette ash and a sprinkling of cigarette butts.

Thinking back I had never seen Hoight smoking, and I had never detected the smell of cigarettes on him. So logically he had a semi-permanent girlfriend who smoked Camels during breakfast and after sex. Perhaps during sex too. Who knew?

Then I spotted the scrunched piece of paper. I had fished out a few receipts from the Mott Haven Deli and St. Anne's Café Restaurant, but this was not a receipt. It was bigger and the paper was heavier. I picked it up and spread it out on the work surface. It was a note. There were grease stains and smudges of ketchup on it, but the writing was still legible. It was the big, unformed hand of somebody who was unaccustomed to writing. It was a childish hand with big loops and letters of unequal size.

You wuz still sleeping when I went out. I hadda go to work. U still owe me fifty bucks and twenty for the chow last night, I need it today, so dont keep me fuckin wating. Today Im on Tiffany, up by the monastry gardens. You better get the do to me befor you go to yor fuckin meetin. Be there befor seven of Fraz is gonna break my jaw. You no he dun that befor, so don't foget.
Candy

Her name was Candy, she smoked Camel cigarettes and needed seventy bucks before seven PM.

I went down, loped over to the 7-Eleven on the corner, with my shoulders hunched, and bought a couple of packs of Camels and a pint of tequila.

It was a short drive to Hunts Point, and fifteen minutes later I turned off Lafayette onto Tiffany and started a slow crawl down past the monastery gardens, where the enclosed trees towered, russet and fading green over the ugly gray concrete walls. There were not many girls. It was not only wet, it was early too, and the dark appetites tend to come out in the secret hours, after the sun has gone. But there was a small group huddled against the wall by the lamppost, just before the dilapidated house at 754. It might be raining and turning cold, but their pimps wanted their dough.

I did a U-turn and rolled up beside them, sliding down the window and leaning across the passenger seat to call to them. They noticed me and tried not to look bored while offering me views of their cleavages and their legs that were more bizarre than enticing. I smiled.

"I'm looking for Candy."

They closed in. One girl, chewing gum like she was in a gum-chewing exhibition, cocked her hip and said, "How come?"

"Brad asked me to drop by. He wanted me to give her something. Are you Candy?"

She looked back at a pretty black girl under a pink plastic umbrella, with frizzy hair and a broken nose. The girl looked nervous. "Brad asked you to drop by?"

"Yeah. You Candy? He hasn't been here already, has he? He told me he had a meeting and he couldn't make it."

The girl who wouldn't admit she was Candy came closer. "No, he ain't bin here. What he want you to give her?"

"He said he owed you fifty bucks..."

Now she had either to accept fifty bucks and get her jaw broken again, or admit she was Candy and tell me it was seventy. There was no contest. She snapped, "Seventy! That son of a bitch owes me seventy, not fifty."

I grinned. "My mistake." I handed her seventy bucks. She snatched the money, then smiled when I showed her another fifty and a paper bag with a bottle of tequila and two packs of Camels.

She said, "You want a little something while you're here?"

"Sure, hop in where it's dry and warm. Brad said you're fun to be with."

"He said that?"

She pulled open the passenger door and climbed in. "Whatcha got in mind?"

I pulled away and turned right onto Lafayette Avenue. I glanced at her as the lights from the streetlamps washed over her. I grinned. "Somewhere quiet, a candlelit dinner for two, the moon over the sea, just you and me..."

She gaped and then laughed. "You're funny. If you wanna take me somewhere an' take your time, that's extra. My Fraz sets the prices. That's nothin' to do with me."

"I'm not bothered about the price, Candy. I just want to know about Brad's meeting today."

She went very still. "Why?"

"You known Brad long?"

She shrugged. "Couple of years."

"He talk to you a lot?"

"You know how it is with some guys. Sometimes they prefer to talk than screw."

"Really? I wouldn't know. So he must have talked to you about McDonald."

She didn't answer straight away. I glanced at her. She said, "You a cop?"

I laughed like what she'd said was funnier than she knew. "No, honey, I ain't a cop. I'm a friend of Brad's and I'm worried he's going to do something stupid." I glanced at her again. She still looked uncertain. "He ever talk to you about McDonald?"

"No, not really. Sometimes lately when he was high, or drunk, he started saying weird things about how everything was gonna change when he squared McDonald's debt."

"Yeah, well, I think he has arranged a meeting today with somebody who does not want him to square that debt. And I need to find him before it's too late."

"What's your name?"

The question surprised me. I glanced at her a moment and said, "Jay, why?"

"Jay?" She pulled the corners of her mouth down and shrugged. "He never talked about a friend called Jay."

We'd reached the intersection with Drake Street and Edgewater Road. I crossed over to the garden by the river and killed the engine. I pulled a hundred bucks from my wallet and showed her the wad.

"Problem is, Candy, I haven't got the time to prove to you that I am his friend. So that leaves you with two possibilities. One: I am here as his friend and I genuinely do want to help him, or two: I am his enemy and I want to hurt him, or worse still, maybe kill him. Now you have to think, if one is right and you don't tell me where he is, not only does Brad get hurt and maybe even killed by the person he's having his meeting with, but you also miss out on your hundred and fifty bucks, having achieved nothing by not telling me. On the other hand, if one is a lie and two is right, that means right now you are sitting alone in a car with a very dangerous man—and you are refusing to cooperate with him and tell him what he wants to know. A fact which could make him real mad. So not only are you putting your own life at risk, you are also putting your friends who saw you leave with me at risk because, if I am a very bad man, I will have to go back and silence them, too, as potential witnesses. So if I were you, Candy, I would think positive. I would take the money, the tequila and the cigarettes, and trust that I am who I say I am, and I will do my very best to help Brad."

She stared at me with a perfectly blank face for a long moment. Then blinked and smiled. "I guess I got no choice, right?"

"Right."

"OK. You want something else before you take me back?"

SIXTEEN

The most she could tell me was that he had said something about having to go to Pelham Bay Park. A gut feeling told me I knew what that meant. I dropped Candy back to huddle with her friends on Tiffany, and took the Bruckner Expressway east toward the country club and Pelham Bay. At Exit 7C I came off onto the Bruckner Boulevard which I followed through gentle, damp suburbia onto Middletown Road, and shortly after that I parked in the parking lot by the stadium, opposite Huntington Woods.

I sat there, drumming my fingers on the steering wheel and watching the heavy, dark clouds. They had broken briefly to show that the sky was still blue above, and the sun was still shining. But now they were closing in again, shutting out the light. A few heavy drops tapped, desultory, on the windshield. I climbed out, locked the truck and took a stroll around the lot. It didn't take me long to find his cream Taurus.

At the exit to the parking lot there was a footpath. I followed it left, crunching on russet leaves and smelling the damp earth from the forest. The breeze was turning chill. I passed the police stables and turned right along the edge of the ballpark, in among the encroaching woodland, until I came to the rocky shore of the bay. The smell of ozone was strong. Tall grass and large rocks peppered the muddy edge of the water, where small, desultory waves lapped in a broken rhythm. A gust made the trees sigh and bow behind me. There was no sign of Hoight. So I started to walk along the damp shore, picking my way among reeds, shrubs, rock pools and weathered stones, with the blustery breeze throwing cold spots of rain in my face.

I came to a narrow, beaten path and turned in, toward the trees. Shrubs soon gave way to saplings, which in turn gave way to hickory, oaks and maples. The gray light of the gray day faded further as the trees closed in, and in the dark the sound of my boots in the undergrowth was both muffled, contained among the trees and the ferns, and magnified by them.

After three or four minutes I came to a small glade. A dead tree lay across it and an overgrown path led away through saplings back toward the sea. Hoight was sitting against the large, prone tree trunk, watching me. He had his legs stretched out in front of him, crossed at the ankle, and his hands in his lap, holding the Smith and Wesson .22. His right hand was bandaged halfway up his forearm. The drizzle had matted his hair and it was sticking in strands to his forehead. As I drew closer I saw that the drops were running into his eyes, but he wasn't blinking. He was very pale and waxy, and when I hunkered down and touched his face he was cold.

The cause of death was not immediately apparent, but after a moment I found the slim incision just behind his left collarbone. It's one of the fastest, cleanest ways to kill a person. With the right blade, it severs the aorta, the carotid artery and punctures the heart itself. And if the blow is delivered correctly, all the massive hemorrhaging occurs internally. Death comes in seconds. But because of the location, it is a very difficult blow to deliver, especially cleanly. This one was spotless.

The drizzle was growing heavier. I could hear it tapping on the leaves overhead, but it wasn't loud enough to cover the soft footfall fifty feet behind me. I wiped the moisture from my brow and from my eyes and stood.

"What are you doing here, Harry?"

I didn't turn. I'd been aware he was behind me since I'd reached the shore, but I hadn't heard the cocking of a pistol or the click of a hammer, so I'd decided to wait. I spoke, still looking down at Hoight's body.

"I was going to ask you the same question, Corporal. Has the brigadier got you following me?"

"No."

I turned. He was as I had seen him that night. Jeans, black leather jacket, his hands in his jacket pockets. "So?"

"You first, Harry."

"I was looking for Hoight."

"Looks like you found him."

"Somebody else found him first."

"Yeah? Might be wise to move out. People walk their dogs round here."

"Did you kill him, Corporal?"

"Why would I want to kill that poor tosser?"

"I don't know. But he has a gun in his lap which should be with our forensics team. Last time I saw it, you were going to take it there."

He became very still. "Maybe it was one of a pair."

"Maybe. So I told you why I'm here. Now you."

He smiled and shook his head. "Nah, Harry. It's not that easy, mate. How about you tell me how you knew he'd be here?"

I didn't speak for a moment. I just listened to all the wet, forest sounds around me. There were no snuffling dogs, no crunching, tramping feet.

"How come I need to give you any kind of explanation at all, Corporal, for whatever the hell I am doing? How is what I do any of your goddamn business?"

"That's the way it works, Harry, me old mucker. We all look

out for each other. Now, you tell me how you knew this poor wanker was here, and I'll tell you why *I'm* here."

"I went to his office, I went to his apartment, and eventually found my way to his girlfriend. She told me he had an appointment at Pelham Bay. I found his car in the lot and then just followed a hunch. You want to have a private meeting, this is as good a place as any in New York. So I nosed around and found him here dead, with you in the trees. Your turn."

"I was told to tail him. Your museum piece got a hit on AFIS *and* CODIS. The brigadier obviously told you about that. Brad Hoight, a private dick. He had some form. Nothing to write home about, but enough to make him interesting to us. Petty theft, bit of harmless extortion, small-time blackmail; but most of all acts of random violence. Chief thought it was a sign of an unbalanced man. Thought maybe he had become fixated on you.

"When we ran the registration number of the revolver and it turned out it had belonged to Gregorio McDonald as part of his collection, the coincidence was a bit too much. He'd taken Gregorio's name and his gun, and he was stalking you. The chief wanted to know why." He gave a small shrug. "So here I am, following him."

I looked back at the body. "So if you didn't kill him, who did?" I looked back at the corporal. "That is not an easy kill. It takes skill. The kind of skill you have."

"Don't be modest, Harry. You have those same skills yourself."

"Yeah, but I just got here. You were supposed to be watching him."

"I was. Like I said, he was a private dick. So I had to be careful tailing him. As you well know, creeping through the woods is a noisy business unless you are slow, careful and patient. So he pulled ahead, and by the time I got here, he was dead." He nodded at the corpse. "Just the way you see him now."

"Whoever he came to see killed him?"

"That's the way it looks to me. Any suggestions?" There was just a hint of irony in his voice.

"I had no reason to kill him. All I wanted was information. Information I am now not going to get." We stood a moment staring at each other, sizing each other up, till I asked him the question that was nagging at my mind.

"So why do you care if I killed him or not?"

He shrugged. "Personally, I don't give a shit, mate. But the chief likes a tight ship. One thing is delivering on a contract. Quite another is going out and performing an unsolicited public service. Rules are strict on that one."

"So were you following him or me?"

He shrugged. "Let's say I was keeping an eye on both of you."

"He told you I might kill Hoight?"

He smiled and shook his head. "Nah, not him. Her."

A cold anger suffused my skin. "The colonel?"

He was enjoying it and made no attempt to hide it. "Yeah, mate, the chief of operations. She was worried you might off the little fucker 'coz he was harassing you."

"The colonel told you to watch me in case I tried to murder Hoight."

"Yes, Harry."

"And what are you going to report to her, Corporal?"

"That you arrived after he was killed, and that you were unwilling to tell me why you had come to find him."

I snarled, "I told you, I wanted to talk to him."

"What about, Harry? The skills you picked up murdering prisoners in Afghanistan?"

I didn't answer for a moment. Then I crossed the distance that separated us. He was an inch taller than me, with powerful shoulders. He didn't move. He kept his eyes on mine.

"You got some beef with me?"

He gave his head a small shake. "I didn't know who you were till the colonel told me."

"You're SAS? I don' remember you."

"Corporal Phil Turner, SAS. We never met."

"You want to know what I wanted to talk to him about?"

"I can't wait, Harry."

"See, the guy who's been harassing me has skills. Real skills. He scaled my house and got into my attic without my noticing, he disabled my alarm system, he got into my room without waking me up. He could have killed me and I would never have known. There aren't many men on this planet who can do that, Corporal. You know that. You're the same."

I let the words sink in a moment, but he had understood. I gave my head a small shake.

"Hoight was not one of those men. He went to pieces under pressure. He was slow and clumsy, and overly emotional. But if I had to point to a man who probably did have those skills, I'd point to you. I think you have those skills and some to spare. What do you say, Corporal?"

"I'd say you're probably right, Harry."

"Did the colonel send you to try and spook me? Was this some kind of stupid test?"

"You'd have to ask her that, wouldn't you? I can't discuss my mission parameters with you."

I stepped close, so there were just inches between us. "You go tell the colonel she got it wrong, again. I am not a murderer, or a common criminal. I do my job how I see fit. You tell her if she has questions for me she can damn-well come and ask me to my face! And you tell her the next time she sends some intruder into my house, I will exercise my right under the law and I will gut him and throw him out of the goddamn window."

He didn't look impressed. He looked mildly amused. I gave my head a small shake.

"Don't bother. I'll go tell her myself."

I brushed past him and headed back through the soft, cold rain, the way I'd come. His voice stopped me at the edge of the clearing.

"Sergeant Bauer."

I stopped dead and turned back, frowning. "Corporal?"

"I have often wanted to ask you, why didn't you intervene at Al-Landy? Why did you do nothing, and just let those people be massacred?"

I went cold. A trickle of cold water ran down the back of my neck. "Son of a bitch."

An old colleague, the brigadier had said.

"I mean, you could have done something, right?"

"There was nothing we could do."

"I heard there were children, raped and murdered."

"All of them."

"While you just lay there and watched."

"If we had moved in..."

"They'd been feeding you, right? The villagers. They'd been risking their lives, leaving food and water out for you. And that was part of what got them killed."

"They were killed because they had installed a TV in a café."

He shook his head. "I don't know how you were able to do it. Just lie there, in the sand, and watch it happen."

"You'd better shut your mouth, Corporal. You'd better stop talking. We were a squad. There were four of us. There were over a hundred Taliban, armed with RPGs and heavy machine guns. If we'd moved in they would have killed us in minutes and then proceeded to massacre the village anyway. We had a mission to search and destroy high-value targets. Which we went on to do, and then we caught ben-Amini. Don't ever talk to me about that subject again, Corporal. You know fuck all about it."

"You're wrong."

"What?"

"I had a friend in that village. A little girl of four. The following month would have been her fifth birthday. We'd pass by that way sometimes and I would take her chocolate. You must have seen her. Because, you were watching while she was raped and murdered."

I could barely hear my voice when I answered him. "There was nothing I could have done."

He nodded. "Right. Well, I've told you now, haven't I? got it off my chest. So there's no fear of my breaking into your house or stalking you. But Sergeant? If ever it came to it, and you tried to gut me and throw me out of the window, I wouldn't be overconfident about the outcome, if I was you."

I turned and walked away with my heart pounding. When I got to the Land Rover I called the brigadier.

"Yes, Harry."

"Brad Hoight is dead."

"Did you kill him?"

"No! Goddammit, sir! I am not a murderer! I am a soldier! I do not go around murdering every damned asshole who happens to piss me off!"

He was quiet for a moment. "I didn't say you were."

"Where is the colonel, sir? Is she still in New York or did she go back to DC?"

"She's still here. Why? What is this about, Harry?"

"She detailed Corporal Phil Turner to watch me and make sure I didn't murder Hoight. I think she ordered him to break into my house too. He has the skills, which I never believed Hoight had. Hoight had some private beef with me, that had to do with McDonald, that's obvious. But he could never have got into my bedroom without waking me. He could never have moved the way that intruder moved. That was Turner under the colonel's instructions."

"That is one hell of an allegation, Harry."

"Turner told me as much just ten minutes ago."

"This thing has got to stop between you two."

"There is no 'between,' sir," I growled. "I did my job and I wanted to talk to Hoight to see why the hell he was stalking me. It turns out the one who was stalking me and breaking into my house was working on the colonel's orders because she now believes I am a homicidal maniac!"

"All right, calm down, Harry. I'll talk to her and arrange a meeting. Make yourself available this evening."

"Sir, I will make myself available, but if I don't get a call in the next couple of hours, I will find her myself and drag her to HQ in Pleasantville and have her tell you and me what the *hell* she is doing. And while I am at it, sir, tell the colonel to tell Corporal Turner that the next time he mentions Al-Landy to me, I am going to shove his head so far up his ass he'll be looking through his own mouth!"

"All right, Harry. Enough. Go home. I'll be in touch in the next couple of hours."

SEVENTEEN

I climbed into the truck and slammed the door, and sat a while trying to relax and drumming on the steering wheel, watching the grayness grow wetter outside.

There are a lot of problems with women. The worst one is that they infect you with their craziness and suddenly, before you know it, you can't think straight anymore and you lose the ability to see what is right in front of your nose.

I pressed the ignition, rolled out of the parking lot and headed back slowly toward the City. My mind went back to that night when I awoke, aware that somebody was there in my room. I remembered lying very still, trying to appear like I was sleeping. I always have the drapes and the window open, but he had managed to close them without waking me. That meant he had stood a foot or two from me and I had not sensed him.

And when I had slipped from the bed, hunkered down and peered around the end of the bed, he was gone. He had left in absolute silence. That is a skill, a very hard skill to master. I wasn't sure I had mastered it completely.

I remembered going after him down the stairs with the P226 in my hand. I remembered the ghostly light from the stained-glass window and the shadow that moved across it. I froze the image in my mind. Outside the car, gray, wet mist rose between the moving vehicles, but in my mind all I could see was the frame-by-frame image of that shadow moving in the dull, stained-glass light.

I had checked every bedroom on the second floor one by one, starting by the stairs and moving along the landing. I had seen nothing, heard nothing. Yet he had been there, watching me. He could have killed me in my bed, he could have killed me then, as I searched for him, but he hadn't. Because the colonel had told him not to.

I felt a hot surge of rage and betrayal in my belly. So if he was not supposed to kill me, what *was* he supposed to do? Spy on me? To prove what?

I had sprung after him, bellowing, "*Stop! Stop goddammit!*"

I saw him in my memory, just a few feet ahead of me, vaulting the banisters in a single, fluid movement. I remembered him in the clearing, strong, powerful, confident. I remembered him walking away from the stoop, back toward the van, the same powerful confidence in his movements. I recognized the hot madness of jealousy eating at the edges of my reason and fought to control it. But the truth was there to be seen. I had risked my life, traveled halfway across the world to find her and save her, and she, in her gratitude, had refused to see me, refused even to attend briefings with me, and had now taken up with this damned thug to spy on me.

"God dammit!" I pounded the wheel and bellowed without realizing it. "That *stupid*, damned woman!"

I had just passed under Castle Hill Avenue and was approaching Exit 53, when my cell rang. It was the brigadier.

"Yeah!"

"Where are you?"

"Bruckner Expressway, approaching exit fifty-three. Headed home."

I had a sudden, overwhelming urge to be with Angel, pack a couple of cases, bundle her in the TVR and escape to Vermont for a month in bed and huge log fires, with the occasional walk through drifts of autumn leaves.

"Take the exit. Come to headquarters at Pleasantville. The colonel is here. I hope you arrive ready to resolve this once and for all. This situation between you two ends today."

"I was ready to do that a long time ago, sir. I hope you are ready to accept my resignation. Because I have had just about a bellyful of this BS."

"Keep your hair on, Harry. Please let at least two of us behave like adults."

I grunted and hung up. At the exit I came off onto the Bruckner Boulevard and just after Soundview I made the three big loops and took the Bronx River Parkway north, with a bitter anger in my gut, resigned to the fact that after I had been through hell and back to save her neck, the colonel had finally managed to kick me out of COBRA.

It took me just over half an hour to get there, but as late afternoon was turning to copper I turned up Apple Hill Lane and made my way to the large, iron gates that gave onto the sweeping parkland and apple orchards that surrounded, and camouflaged, COBRA HQ.

I drove up the winding, gravel drive and came finally to a genuine English Jacobean manor house which some crazy tycoon had shipped over brick by brick in the 1920s, gables, tall chimneys and all.

I was admitted electronically to a stone-flagged hallway, about ten-foot square. The walls were stone too. Directly in front of me there was another, massive wooden door with a screen and a keypad on the wall beside it. I punched in a code and six green lasers scanned my face and my eyes. There was a metallic clunk and the door swung inward.

I was met by a butler in a white coat who smiled and bowed and said, "Please follow me."

I did and he led me through a large lobby with a checkerboard floor and high ceilings supported on wooden rafters. We climbed an elegant staircase up to the next floor. There, down a red-carpeted corridor, he tapped on a wooden door and, without waiting, opened it and stepped in.

"Mr. Bauer, sir."

I knew the study. I had been there before. It had all the Old World elegance of the brigadier and smelled of open fires, furniture polish and pipe tobacco. Books lined the walls on dark wooden bookcases, leather armchairs and sofas stood on genuine Persian rugs, and tall, leaded, gabled windows overlooked sweeping green lawns.

The colonel was sitting in one of those chesterfields, staring at the dancing flames in the grate. She had a glass of whisky in her hand. She didn't look at me.

Over by the window the brigadier rose from behind his desk, smiled and crossed the room to shake my hand.

"Harry, come on in, take a seat by the fire. Drink?"

"Thanks."

He poured me a generous measure from a decanter and another for himself, and we both sat either side of the colonel, by the fire. She didn't move but continued to stare at the flames. I made a question with my eyebrow and looked at the brigadier. He said:

"You are both aware why we are here, and I am afraid we are going to stay here until this problem is resolved one way or another. Now, before we get started, I am going to lay some ground rules, which will be observed by all of us. I want to hear from both of you, and there will be no interrupting, bullying or pulling of rank, except by me." A ghost of a smile that did not invite a smile in return. "You are both valued, and invaluable, members of my staff, but I am afraid that over the last few months there has been behavior from both of you which has been frankly adolescent. It has to end, here, today. I need you both back working and professional."

He waited. I gave a single nod. The colonel continued to stare at the fire. The brigadier addressed me.

"Harry, I believe you have something to say."

I wanted to thank him for giving me a glimpse of what his prep school must have been like. Instead I turned to the colonel.

"I had a talk with Corporal Phil Turner. I believe he killed Brad Hoight in Huntington Woods. He told me that you, Colonel, had instructed him to follow me. He told me you liked to run a tight ship, that delivering on a contract was one thing, and another was, and I quote, 'performing an unsolicited public service.' He told me that you, Colonel, were worried that I might be doing that, delivering unsolicited public services, and that I might do that to Hoight. So what? You had him killed so I wouldn't murder him?"

I saw her jaw move, like she was going to say something, but I cut in.

"I haven't quite finished yet, Colonel. He said you were worried I might kill Hoight because he was harassing me." I took a second to repress the hot anger that was brewing in my gut. "I believe your...," I bit hard on my teeth for a moment, "...your—I am not really sure what to call him, Colonel—your Corporal Phil Turner, has reported to you that I did not kill Hoight. That Hoight was already dead when I arrived. So," I could not keep the bitterness from my voice, "whoever the murderer is, Colonel, it is not me. The only other person I know of who was there was your Phil."

Now her head turned slightly and her eyes swiveled to look at me. I met her eye and let her see the anger and the betrayal I felt. She turned back to the fire.

"I am almost done. I have to mention the fact that he also raised the issue of my wanting to execute Mohammed ben-Amini in Afghanistan, and I don't know where he got that information from. After he had mentioned that, he also accused me and my squad of cowardice for not intervening in the Al-Landy massacre. Again, I don't know how he knew I was there, or whether that view of me as a coward is something you both share and discuss."

The brigadier cleared his throat, like he was warning me of something, and the colonel turned and glared at me.

"So here are the things I want to know, Colonel. One," I held up my index finger, "why you sent your Phil..."

She snapped, "*Stop* calling him that!"

The brigadier said, "Enough, Harry. That is not relevant."

I gave him a look that said maybe it wasn't relevant to him and turned back to the colonel. "Why you sent...Corporal Phil Turner...to keep an eye on me and why you told him you were afraid I would perform an 'unsolicited public service.' Two," I made the V sign, "why you sent him to spook me in my house. What were you trying to do between you, prove what a coward I was? Prove what a homicidal maniac I was? Because I would have thought you had all the proof you needed, to show my cowardice and my homicidal tendencies, when I chased you halfway around the world trying to save your ass!"

She closed her eyes and clenched her upper lip with her teeth. I went on.

"And three," I held up my thumb with my two fingers, "why did you have him kill Hoight? Were you trying to frame me? Was your purpose all along, with all of this *stupid* game, to have me kicked out of COBRA? Because I have to tell you, you have been wasting company money. All you had to do was ask me to leave and I would have left. In fact it is what I intend to do when this meeting is over."

I sat back in my chair and took a swig of whisky. The brigadier cleared his throat again.

"Harry, have you said everything you wanted to say?"

I drew breath to say I had, but in the end I shook my head and said, "No. I have one last thing I need to say. On a personal note. I feel badly betrayed by somebody I considered not just a colleague, but an ally and a friend."

They both frowned, like echoes of each other, and a heavy silence fell on the room. Eventually she said, "I am sorry you feel that way. I mean it. Genuinely."

I gave a small laugh. "How would you feel if the brigadier did to you what you have just done to me?"

"Harry." It was the brigadier. "You've had your say. It is Jane's turn to talk."

I sighed and nodded. She went on.

"In answer to your last question, I imagine I would feel the way you do. But there is a difference, Harry. I don't go around blowing things up all the time. Do you realize that the body count on your jobs is three times higher, that is *three hundred percent higher*, than any other operative we use?"

"How about the success rate? What's the percentage on that?"

"Shut up, Harry!" The brigadier fixed me with his eye. "I won't tell you again."

"The success rate is also higher. But I have to tell you that it worries me. Both your success rate and the...," she hesitated, "the sheer *violence* with which you undertake the missions. You are not an assassin, Harry. You're a war zone. I know you say you are not a ninja, you are a soldier, but it worries me." She paused, staring at the fire again, then, "Not just because it could so easily kick back on COBRA." She looked at me. "We are supposed to be covert, you know. Low profile is important for an agency like ours. But you get noticed, and that could damage us in the end. But it's not just that, I worry for you. Harry, whatever you may believe, I *am* your friend and your ally. But there is so much violence and aggression inside you. I don't know what to make of you."

She sipped her whisky and took a moment. I watched the flames in her glass twist and flicker.

"I certainly have not been trying to prove you a coward or a homicidal maniac. I know you are anything but a coward. As you rather unnecessarily pointed out, I have good reason to know that you are a very brave man. And homicidal maniac is overly dramatic and sensational. What I am not so sure about is how much self-control you have. You killed John Martinez. There was no contract on him. You killed him because you didn't like the fact that he was trying to extort your...," she took a deep breath and said, woodenly, "your new girlfriend. Your personal feelings and your emotions get tangled up with your work, Harry. And I can't help worrying about it." Another deep breath. "Having said that, I repeat, I certainly do not believe you are a coward or a homicidal maniac."

She took another swig and stared into her glass as she swallowed, like she might have lost something in there

"I believe that answers your first question. But I want to stress, that Corporal Turner is by no stretch of the imagination 'my Phil,' and I resent the implication. As you know very well, Harry, I keep my personal relationships completely separate from my work. If Corporal Turner knows about ben-Amini and Al-Landy I assure you that has absolutely nothing to do with me."

The brigadier cut in, looking at me. "I will look into that, Harry, and I assure you, you will have no more trouble from Turner."

I nodded. "Thanks." I turned back to the colonel. There was no warmth in my expression when I asked her, "And what about my other two questions?"

EIGHTEEN

She stood and walked away from us to the tall, narrow leaded window and stood gazing out at the silent, ochre and russet trees, the gray sky and the wet lawn.

"I didn't," she said after a moment. "The brigadier told me you needed someone to keep an eye on the house. I sent a team and they were killed. So the brigadier told me to select a team with a background with either Delta, SBS or SAS. I chose Turner and three other men he often worked with. He has an impressive résumé. I certainly did not give him instructions to spook you." She turned and looked at me. "And I *certainly* did not want to prove that you were a coward or a homicidal maniac. While I am on the subject, I deeply resent the implication that Turner and I have some kind of close relationship. I hardly know the man, and I would have to be insane to develop such a convoluted plot. You are one of our most valuable assets, and besides, if I felt you were no longer of value to COBRA I would first discuss it with the brigadier, and then we would both discuss it with you and invite you to resign on a very generous pension. That would be the normal thing."

The brigadier sighed. "Jane, can you offer any thoughts on

why Turner would imply, as Harry says he did, that you had ordered him to spook Harry in his house?"

She came back and leaned on the back of her chair. "Yes," she said, "I can. Knowing men like Turner and Harry, I can quite easily visualize them beating their chests and spewing pheromones and testosterone all over Huntington Woods, and I would imagine that Harry was probably supremely aggressive and menacing." She turned to me and raised a hand. "Which is understandable after what you had been through, and fresh from the job in Montauk."

I didn't say anything. I just blinked and she went on.

"But I would imagine that faced with a situation like that, Corporal Turner probably responded by doing his best to aggravate Harry still further."

The brigadier turned to me. "Feasible?"

I shrugged and looked back at the colonel.

She said, "I would find it very hard to believe that the corporal would have killed the original team who were watching your house. Further, as far as I am aware, he has no connection whatever with the Mexicans or Gregorio McDonald, so I can't imagine what his motivation would be."

She came around the chair and sat again. She was quiet for a while, with her elbows on her knees and her hands clasped, as she watched the flames again.

"Harry, I am aware that since I was abducted, since I got back..." She trailed off, sighed and closed her eyes. "What I am trying to say is that since you, in your words, chased me halfway around the world trying to save my ass, I have been withdrawn, I *have* avoided you and I have not shown my gratitude. That was wrong of me and I apologize. I don't know if you can understand this, but I was too grateful."

She glanced at me. I shook my head and she looked away.

"Well, whether you understand it or not, my distancing myself from you was not a lack of gratitude, nor was it that I disliked you. This is very hard for me to say, but I was deeply grateful, and I admired your courage and your dedication more, perhaps, than I should."

I scowled, frowned at the brigadier and he gave his head a small shake. The colonel went on.

"The bottom line was that, while I had therapy for PTSD, my therapist and I both thought it was best if I did not see you."

I bit back a burst of irritation and tried to suppress a sigh.

"As to having Hoight killed." She turned to look at me. "It would be a bit stupid, wouldn't it, to detail Turner to make sure you didn't kill Hoight, and then have him do the job for you? As far as I am aware, Hoight had not committed any crimes against humanity, so I had no reason to issue a contract on him." She spread her hands and looked back at the fire. "I think that answers all your questions. As I said before, I can imagine that you do feel betrayed, and I am sure I would feel the same way if I were in your shoes. But I have not tried to sabotage you, and I have not tried to get you ejected from COBRA," she paused and hesitated, "neither am I in any kind of relationship with Corporal Turner. What I will hold my hand up to is feeling *very* insecure about the way you operate. Perhaps the failing is mine, not yours."

We all three fell silent. After a moment the brigadier spoke.

"Harry, I realize that Jane's response leaves a couple of questions unanswered, but I think they are questions that she is not in fact in a position to answer..."

I had been silent too long and I interrupted him. "Like who killed the operatives you had watching my house, and who killed Hoight, and why. And why Hoight adopted the surname McDonald, and the meaning of the John Donne poem, 'Each man's death diminishes me, for I am involved in mankind. Therefore, never send to know for whom the bell tolls; it tolls for thee.' Implying that I had to pay for the men I had killed." I sat forward. "There is something I have not told you about Turner. When he raised the subject of Al-Landy, he told me he had a friend in that village, a little girl of four who was raped and murdered by ben-Amini and his thugs. Apparently he and his boys used to pass by the village from time to time, and he would always bring her chocolate."

The brigadier said, "Oh…"

"If he had that grudge against me, if there was a contract out for whoever killed Gregorio McDonald, it's not impossible that Turner would get to hear about it…"

The colonel shook her head. "Let's not jump to conclusions."

The brigadier stood abruptly.

"We have discussed everything which is pertinent to me and to COBRA. As far as that is concerned I take the issue to be closed and resolved and I want to hear no more about it. I have some matters to look into regarding Hoight and Turner. Jane, the matter is out of your hands. I shall deal with it. Now, I believe, you two have personal matters which you need to address."

I groaned quietly, thinking of Angel waiting for me at home. The brigadier collected his coat and his hat and paused before going to the door. "Jane, I shall expect you back on full duty as of tomorrow morning. Harry, you have two weeks' holiday as of tomorrow morning. Get whatever it is off your chest and in November I want you ready for your next job. Good evening to you both."

The door closed behind him and I sat staring at the colonel a moment.

"I don't know about you," I said, "but I don't think we have much to talk about. Apparently, trying to get you back from Gabriel Yushbaev was some kind of unforgivable transgression of your rights as a free, independent woman and since then you have not been able to look at me without feeling disgust at my primitive, animal nature."

"Jesus!" She covered her face with her hands. "You didn't listen to a damn word I said, did you?"

"Sure, I did. I heard you say several times that there was nothing between you and Corporal Turner, and the minute I pointed out he might have a motive to be stalking me, you jumped to his defense like…"

"I did *not* jump to his defense! Christ, Harry! You are impossible when you are like this!"

"Yeah? Well apparently I am like this all the time, because every time I have tried to see you, every time I have tried to talk to you to see how you were, you have cut me dead. Tell me something, was Corporal Turner helping you to get over your PTSD? It's a shame the brigadier didn't send *him* to get you. Maybe his assassinations would have been more exquisitely low profile!"

She was suddenly on her feet. "God! You are such an asshole! What about you and your twenty-year-old protégé? What is it with you, Harry? You didn't come...," her arm jutted out and she pointed vaguely in the direction of DC, "you didn't come and see me and keep asking why I was not at briefings because you *cared* about me! Oh, no! What was eating you, what has always eaten away at your pathetic little ego, was that *I did not sleep with you!* Every little lady that toddles along your way seems to fall helplessly into the sack with you. But I wouldn't, and I won't! And that—*that*—is what you can't stand! You have the effrontery to come here beating your chest, getting all macho and jealous about the corporal, when you are *screwing that hooker!* How *dare* you come on to me like some territorial caveman when you have *another woman* living in your house!"

I got to my feet, feeling all logic and reason turning to dust in my fingers, and half yelled, "Well why the hell wouldn't I? When every time I have tried to get close to you, you cut me dead and whined on about the damn job! What am I supposed to do? Become a monk? Give myself to the sacred cause of Colonel Jane? Never again to have or be had?"

"Don't be so stupid!"

"You know what I mean, Jane! You *know* there was something there between us. You felt it like I did."

She took a step toward me with her hand clenched somewhere between claws and fists.

"For God's sake, Harry! How can you be so dense? Do you really think that any woman who really knew you—" She flung out her arm again, pointing randomly at the world. "Because all these women who pass through your bed like the Rio Carnival, none of them *knows* you. *I* know you! *I* know what you are *really like!* Do you think that any woman in her right mind, knowing what you are *really* like, would ever *dream* of getting involved with you?" We glared at each other in silence before she exploded with, "Yes! You are a hunk. Yes! You are almost irresistibly magnetic and fascinating! Yes, if I were stupid enough to just want sex, I would rip my clothes off right now and jump on you. *But I am not that stupid! And I know that a relationship with you would be a nightmare!*"

I frowned. My brain hurt with the maelstrom of half-finished thoughts and emotions that was churning in my head.

I faltered, then said, "With the right woman, I could be a good man…"

"Don't!" She held out both palms to me and turned away. "Just don't!"

She brushed past me and went to the desk where she grabbed her coat and her handbag. I said, "We haven't finished."

"Oh, we have! Believe me, we have."

"Jane—"

"What?" She was shrugging on her coat.

"You and Turner…?"

Her eyes bulged. "*No! No Harry! No!*" She rolled her eyes up, imploring Heaven for patience. "God! You are so dense!"

She stormed to the door, opened it, went out and slammed it shut. There was an enormous silence left behind in the room. I drained my glass. Gave her ten minutes to get away, and then made my way out to the Land Rover. It was dark, and the drizzle was turning to rain, turning the lights of the old manor house into bizarre abstracts of light on the windshield. I hit the wipers and they creaked across the glass, making things clear for a moment before they became confused and broken again.

I called Angel.

"Hey, where are you? I was getting worried."

"Yeah, things got complicated and I had to attend to...things. But I may have some good news when I get back."

"Yeah? Cool. I can't wait. How long will you be? Shall I start making something special? I could open some wine." She giggled. "I was snooping around and I saw you have some *nice* wines."

"Yeah." I took a deep breath. "That would be good. I'll be half an hour, forty-five minutes maximum."

"Can't wait."

I made my way back down the drive with the headlamps punching big yellow holes in the quickening darkness. The wipers kept up their slow, squeaking dirge. I turned out of the gate and started down the hill toward Pleasantville, to pick up the road back to the City. I had a terrible feeling inside, like something disastrous had happened, something irreversible that was bad, real bad. There was an urgency in my chest to go and try and fix it, but I knew I couldn't. I didn't even know what it was I had to fix.

Eventually I found myself approaching Yonkers. By then it was very dark outside and the rain grew suddenly very heavy, so that all I could see was wet lights, shimmering blacktop and water cascading down the windshield. The traffic slowed to a crawl and the rhythm of the wipers accelerated to a panicking heartbeat. In my mind I heard Ella singing, "We'll go to Yonkers, where true love conquers in the whiles..."

"Come *on!*"

I pounded the steering wheel with my fist and ran my fingers through my hair. Lights flashing ahead and a cop with a flashlight and a long black coat like Batman told me there had been an accident. We crawled by and I saw two mangled cars that had been dragged to the roadside. A woman sitting in the back of an ambulance, a blanket over her shoulders, her face in her hands.

Another voice in my head told me, "*Carpe diem*," seize the day, but what about the night, when it's dark and you don't know which way to go?

The traffic began to move again, the rain eased and pretty soon I was crossing Madison Avenue Bridge and turning onto 5th

Avenue. A few blocks and I was turning into James Baldwin Place and pulling up in front of my house. The living-room drapes were closed, but warm light was spilling out, touching the iron railing and the brownstone stoop. I killed the engine and sat staring for a while. Then I climbed out, closed and locked the doors with a bright bleep, and climbed the steps with the wet drizzle creeping down my neck and my back. I was reaching for the keys in my pocket, but the door opened and she was standing there, small and slight, looking up at me. She had showered and washed her hair, which was thick and black and fluffy. Her bruising was almost gone and her face was beautiful, more for its warm smile than anything else. She was barefoot. had on a pair of jeans and one of my shirts. She held out her arms to me and I took her and held her, and breathed in the delicious smell of her skin. With my foot, I kicked the door closed behind me.

NINETEEN

After a while she led me into the living room, poured me a large whisky and sat beside me on the sofa. She stroked my face and said quietly, "You look exhausted."

"It's been a difficult day."

"You want to talk about it?"

I took a moment to answer. "I want to, but I can't. Maybe one day."

"OK, as long as you know that I am here, and you can tell me anything."

"Thanks."

"You want some food?"

I smiled. "Did you go to a lot of trouble?"

She gave a small laugh. "Not really."

"I don't think I can eat."

"What do you want to do?"

I set down the glass and took her hands. "I want to tell you that tomorrow I am handing in my resignation. As of tomorrow I want to devote my life to two things: I want to start to mend and heal, not just myself but other people too; and I want to devote every moment of every day and night to making you happy. Will you let me do that?"

She put her arms around me and held me. "Yes, Harry. If you will let me help you heal, and find happiness."

We kissed for a long time. Then she stood and took my hand. "Let's go upstairs and make a start."

As I stood my cell rang. She frowned but I took it and saw it was the brigadier.

"Harry, I thought you would like to know. Corporal Turner is on his way in to brief me on what has been happening, but I have made some preliminary inquiries."

"Yeah? And...?"

"He was in Afghanistan at the same time as you. He was in Helmand Province at the same time, also on search and destroy. He had been to Al-Landy. I am also told that there were rumors that an SAS group had witnessed the massacre and had been unable to intervene. I don't want to make any hasty judgments, but it is beginning to look as though Turner may have had a grudge against you."

"What about the two guys you had watching the house?"

"As far as I can tell he was not on duty that night."

"Where is he now?"

"He's on his way to see me."

"OK, you'll let me know the outcome."

"Of course."

She had left me talking in the hall and gone up ahead of me. I put my cell in my pocket and followed her up. When I got to the bedroom she had shed her clothes and pulled back the covers. She held out her arms to me and I approached her. For a while we just stood like that, holding each other. Then she whispered, "Lie down and close your eyes. Let me undress you and give you a massage."

I smiled and she unlaced and eased off my boots and my socks. Then she unbuttoned my shirt and I sat up so she could pull it off. Then she put her finger on my chest and pushed me back. "Lie down and close your eyes while I pull off your jeans."

I flopped back and closed my eyes, acutely aware of every

movement of her hands and her fingers. She pulled off my pants with a giggle and then I felt her body close and warm beside me. That was when I opened my eyes and snatched her wrist in my hand.

She gasped. Her eyes were wide with shock. In her right hand she had a long, very slim stiletto, poised just above my left collarbone.

We stared at each other for a long moment. She looked small, naked and vulnerable.

"Is that the same one you used on Hoight, or was it a special one just for me?"

"This one was just for you."

"It belonged to your dad."

She nodded. Then her face crumpled and twisted. "You took him away from me. I loved him so much and you stole him from me."

I wanted to tell her it hadn't been me, but I couldn't, because it had been me as much as it had been Rusanov or any member of his gang. And in my mind I was seeing the crying girl, just four years old, crying over her dead father. I could have asked her about all the orphaned children that her father had left in his wake, but it would have made no difference. It would not have eased the terrible pain she felt inside.

All I could do was take the exquisite, razor-sharp blade from her fingers and drop it on the floor. As I stood she clung to me, wrapped her arms around me and sobbed into my chest. I felt the wetness of her tears on my skin as I embraced her. I told her, over and again, "I am sorry, I am so sorry," while she repeated over and again, one simple word, "*Daddy, Daddy, Daddy...*"

MUCH LATER, in the small hours, as the private ambulance pulled away and carried Maria McDonald away to a private hospital in the Catskills, I sat on the stoop with a glass of Macallan in my hand, and Colonel Jane Harris sitting by my side.

"When did you know?"

"Almost from the start. You and your pal Turner threw me off track for a while, but it would only be her. She was small and slight, but then so was Bruce Lee. And though she had skills, they were all about being silent, fast and agile. The intruder never confronted me in a fight. She always fled from confrontation.

"She was a supreme manipulator of people. She used Johnny Martinez so she could meet me apparently by accident. She probably paid the punk to attack her and make it look real. And before that she employed Hoight to find me, but she also seduced him so she could set him up in the frame; so all my suspicions would be focused on him instead of her. God knows what she promised him. She set him up so he would be in my study and I would find him, but it was her who let him in."

"How do you know?"

"I slipped a piece of black plastic from a Styrofoam tray from the groceries, under the attic door when I slipped the deadbolts. Whatever skills you have, you can't open a deadbolt from the wrong side of the door. After I caught Hoight in my study, I checked the attic door, and the piece of black plastic had been dislodged. That meant he had entered that way, the way she had entered, from the back of the house and up over the roof, but only she could have let him in the skylight, or through the door. She was the only one in the house.

"Like the note she left me saying I had been lusting after my victim. The note had been printed. The only way that could have been done was before she came. So the only person who could have known we were going to eat together was her.

"The two operatives watching my house were killed with a .22. There were no casings at the scene. It made sense it was the same .22 revolver, one of a pair, she had got from her father. That's an assumption, but I'm pretty sure the tests will confirm it.

"Then there was the fact that there had been two women in Hoight's apartment before he was killed. One was Candy, his girl-friend, who had made no effort to hide her presence. But the other woman, who had shared his bed, had tried to hide all evidence that she had been there. It made sense it was Angel—Maria."

I sighed. "She wanted me to pay. More than that, she wanted me to know how much she had suffered when she lost her father. So she wanted me to love her first, and then kill me."

We sat in silence for a while. Then she asked me, "Did you love her?"

"It's hard to love someone when you are ninety percent certain they want to kill you. But I did feel sorry for her. I could see she was a lost soul right from the start." I glanced at her and smiled. "I'm glad the brigadier told you to come deal with this."

She shrugged. "He didn't. That was a lie. I *am* the head of operations. This is my job."

"Right. Well, as long as you're on the job, you want one for the road?"

She nodded a few times but made no move to get up. "Harry, the things I said..."

"I know. You don't need to say it. What's that Shakespeare thing? Hard work doth make fools of us all?"

She shook her head. "No."

"Uhh... Stress! Stress doth make fools of us all."

She laughed. "Stop. Let's go get that nightcap."

And we left the New York fall moon gazing down on my stoop, a little disapprovingly, and we went inside and closed the door.

DON'T MISS ANYTHING!

If you want to stay up to date on all new releases in this series, with this author, or with any of our new deals, you can do so by joining our newsletters below.

In addition, you will immediately gain access to our entire *Right House VIP Library,* which includes many riveting Mystery and Thriller novels for your enjoyment!

righthouse.com/email

(Easy to unsubscribe. No spam. Ever.)

ALSO BY BLAKE BANNER

Up to date books can be found at:
www.righthouse.com/blake-banner

ROGUE THRILLERS
Gates of Hell (Book 1)
Hell's Fury (Book 2)

ALEX MASON THRILLERS
Odin (Book 1)
Ice Cold Spy (Book 2)
Mason's Law (Book 3)
Assets and Liabilities (Book 4)
Russian Roulette (Book 5)
Executive Order (Book 6)
Dead Man Talking (Book 7)
All The King's Men (Book 8)
Flashpoint (Book 9)
Brotherhood of the Goat (Book 10)
Dead Hot (Book 11)
Blood on Megiddo (Book 12)
Son of Hell (Book 13)

HARRY BAUER THRILLER SERIES
Dead of Night (Book 1)
Dying Breath (Book 2)
The Einstaat Brief (Book 3)
Quantum Kill (Book 4)
Immortal Hate (Book 5)
The Silent Blade (Book 6)
LA: Wild Justice (Book 7)

Breath of Hell (Book 8)
Invisible Evil (Book 9)
The Shadow of Ukupacha (Book 10)
Sweet Razor Cut (Book 11)
Blood of the Innocent (Book 12)
Blood on Balthazar (Book 13)
Simple Kill (Book 14)
Riding The Devil (Book 15)
The Unavenged (Book 16)
The Devil's Vengeance (Book 17)
Bloody Retribution (Book 18)
Rogue Kill (Book 19)
Blood for Blood (Book 20)

DEAD COLD MYSTERY SERIES
An Ace and a Pair (Book 1)
Two Bare Arms (Book 2)
Garden of the Damned (Book 3)
Let Us Prey (Book 4)
The Sins of the Father (Book 5)
Strange and Sinister Path (Book 6)
The Heart to Kill (Book 7)
Unnatural Murder (Book 8)
Fire from Heaven (Book 9)
To Kill Upon A Kiss (Book 10)
Murder Most Scottish (Book 11)
The Butcher of Whitechapel (Book 12)
Little Dead Riding Hood (Book 13)
Trick or Treat (Book 14)
Blood Into Wine (Book 15)
Jack In The Box (Book 16)
The Fall Moon (Book 17)
Blood In Babylon (Book 18)
Death In Dexter (Book 19)
Mustang Sally (Book 20)

A Christmas Killing (Book 21)
Mommy's Little Killer (Book 22)
Bleed Out (Book 23)
Dead and Buried (Book 24)
In Hot Blood (Book 25)
Fallen Angels (Book 26)
Knife Edge (Book 27)
Along Came A Spider (Book 28)
Cold Blood (Book 29)
Curtain Call (Book 30)

THE OMEGA SERIES
Dawn of the Hunter (Book 1)
Double Edged Blade (Book 2)
The Storm (Book 3)
The Hand of War (Book 4)
A Harvest of Blood (Book 5)
To Rule in Hell (Book 6)
Kill: One (Book 7)
Powder Burn (Book 8)
Kill: Two (Book 9)
Unleashed (Book 10)
The Omicron Kill (Book 11)
9mm Justice (Book 12)
Kill: Four (Book 13)
Death In Freedom (Book 14)
Endgame (Book 15)

ABOUT US

Right House is an independent publisher created by authors for readers. We specialize in Action, Thriller, Mystery, and Crime novels.

If you enjoyed this novel, then there is a good chance you will like what else we have to offer! Please stay up to date by using any of the links below.

Join our mailing lists to stay up to date -->
righthouse.com/email
Visit our website --> righthouse.com
Contact us --> contact@righthouse.com

 facebook.com/righthousebooks

x.com/righthousebooks

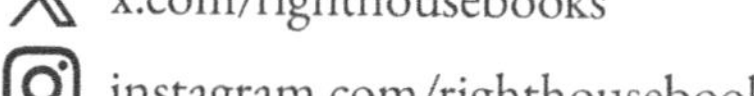 instagram.com/righthousebooks

EXCLUSIVE SNEAK PEAK OF...

BLOOD OF THE INNOCENT

CHAPTER 1

The truck appeared first as a single light glowing in the blackness of the desert, under the immense expanse of stars in the moonless sky. It moved in a slow zigzag, then slowly morphed and split in two, like a luminous amoeba. Gradually it resolved itself into a pair of headlamps whining and grinding along a desert track. They halted and paused where the anonymous dirt track joined State Route 375, in Lincoln County, Nevada. They paused for a couple of seconds, then lumbered right and headed at a steady fifty miles per hour toward Crystal Springs. The truck was a dull red with no markings, and towed a medium-sized trailer. The bill of lading stated the name of the consignor as Edwards Air Force Base, though that was two hundred and fifty miles to the south and west of where the cargo had been collected, at Homey Airport, otherwise known as Groom Lake, or Area 51.

The consignee was listed as the United States Navy, at the Norfolk Navy Yard, 4701 Intrepid Avenue, Norfolk, Virginia. The quantity of cargo was one, the weight was seven tons, the measurements were twelve feet by nine by nine and the volume was nine hundred and seventy-two cubic feet. The description of the cargo was simply, "Sub-aquatic exploration equipment."

At Crystal Springs the truck picked up US Route 93 headed east, and at Panacea, it turned east again to enter Utah, where it finally connected with the I-15 at Cedar City, almost six hours after it had left the base at Groom Lake.

There were four men in the truck, and all were Delta Force operators. They did not wear uniform, nor did they refer to each other by rank. If you weren't fit to lead, they wouldn't follow you, whatever rank you had. Behind the wheel was Black George, six foot six of solid muscle. In the passenger seat was the man they called NY, not because he was from New York, but because he could group thirty-six rounds into a two-inch bull at ninety yards. He had a black beard like a bramble bush and shoulders like two hams.

Traveling in back with the cargo were Scott, who was small, wiry, freckled and rumored to be indestructible, and Twofer, who practiced Zen meditation and was said to have shot two Taliban with a single round, not once but three times.

None of the operators knew what was contained in the metal box in the trailer, though amongst themselves they had concluded it was either EBEs—Extraterrestrial Biological Entities—parts of a captured UAP destined to be reverse engineered at Norfolk, or, least likely according to their assessment, it was an experimental AACC: an Aerial Aquatic Combat Craft, shaped like a giant tic-tac.

From Cedar City the driving became easier, but they didn't pick up the pace much, averaging fifty to sixty miles an hour, and swapping drivers every six hours. At Sulphurdale they turned onto the I-70, went north as far as Salina and then east. They had been driving for some nine hours; it was one thirty AM. NY was at the wheel and they had left the Colorado state line eight miles behind them. They were three miles short of exit 11, for the town of Mack, coming around a broad bend in the road, when they saw the flashing red lights up ahead.

Their orders were strict: stop for nothing and no one until you reach Norfolk. NY didn't slow. Black George pulled his Sig

Sauer P226 from under his arm and spoke into the microphone on his collar.

"We got some kind of barrier in the road up ahead. Red lights, there's a guy in a reflective jacket waving a signal lamp."

The answer came back in his earpiece: "Copy that."

NY said, "There's a truck across the road. I can't get through."

"Shit."

He began to slow. "I either got to ram them or turn around and go back to Utah, pick up the Old US Highway."

"Stop." The two men looked at each other. Black George repeated, "Stop before we get any closer. We need distance if it's a highjack."

NY brought the truck to a halt and reached under his seat for his M4A1 assault rifle. The sixteen-wheeler was fifty or sixty yards up ahead. The cab was facing forward, but the container was angled at forty-five degrees across the road. The guy with the signal lamp had turned his back on them and was facing the distressed truck, where four more men were standing around the cab talking. One of the men appeared to be the sheriff. Black George glanced at the side of the road, by the rear of the sixteen-wheeler. There was a Ford pickup with the Mesa Sheriff's insignia on it.

"Ain't the Mesa Sheriff based at Grand Junction?"

NY nodded. "Yeah, why?"

"We ain't passed Grand Junction yet." He pointed at the Ford. "So how'd he get his pickup this side of the truck?"

The sheriff and the guy with the lamp were walking toward them. Black George said, "Back her up."

There was a sharp, unpleasant noise, like a *spink!* NY let out a soft grunt and sagged. He had a red-black dot in the middle of his forehead, like a Hindu cast mark, and his headrest was spattered with gore. Black George swore violently and spoke into the mic on his collar.

"NY down. We have a hijack."

He grabbed NY's assault rifle, opened the door and dropped to the road. On one knee he double-tapped the guy with the lamp and dropped him. The sheriff was running and the four other guys were training their weapons on him. He double-tapped again and another man went down before a hail of bullets hit the cab. He pulled back and noticed too late the flash of fire from the pickup. Two rounds smacked into him. One into his right eye, the other tore through his chin, ripped open his windpipe and smashed the vertebrae in his neck.

Now the sixteen-wheeler started to straighten up, while four men ran to the back of the hijacked truck. Two heaved open the doors. Staying well behind them, a third covered the door with an automatic rifle from a forty-five-degree angle. The fourth hurled in a gas grenade. The doors were slammed shut again, shutting out the screams of pain from inside as the invisible, odorless VX gas entered the men's bodies, causing violent spasms in their muscles, constricting their chests and causing asphyxia and cardiac arrest in seconds.

Without pause two of the men hauled NY and Black George's bodies into the back of the pickup, then ran to haul open the rear doors of the sixteen-wheeler, lowering a ramp to the blacktop. Meanwhile two more guys clambered into the cab of the high-jacked truck and drove it at speed up the ramp and into the larger container. The Ford pickup followed close behind.

Four minutes after the hit, the sixteen-wheeler was on her way, and the only sign that anything had happened on the road was a small crystal cube of shattered windshield, and by nine AM that morning it was incrusted in the wheel of a Mercedes Benz on its way to Salt Lake City.

The sixteen-wheeler followed the same route NY would have followed as far as Denver, but there, where NY would have continued along the I-70 to Kansas, Indianapolis and Pittsburgh, and then on the I-76 to Norfolk, the sixteen-wheeler took the Colorado I-76 north and east to merge with the I-80 at Ogallala, on the long, uninterrupted journey to New York.

At the wheel was the man in the sheriff's hat. They called him the Cap because he had once been a captain, though he never specified where or of what. He liked to boast that he had lost count of how many people he had killed, and he liked to linger over the word "people," allowing the full implications of the word to filter through.

It was true. At first he had remembered each one of them, and he had wondered what the average was for a special forces operator. It was hard to tell, but he'd figured it was between one and five. So he had strived to achieve six. And along the way he had discovered that it was easier to clock up kills moonlighting in the private sector, especially in Africa, than in the regular army.

When he'd reached eleven kills he had started to lose track of who they were. The women and the kids tended to linger, stirring a vague, emotional uncertainty in his bowels, but the men just kind of blurred into one. And that was ten years ago.

Nowadays, sometimes he thought about his immortal soul, whether he had one, and what awaited it on the other side. But not often. Mostly he just cycled through work, violence, drink, violence and work again.

The truck hummed and the dark road slipped by.

After a while he looked at the man sitting next to him. They called him Seth. Nobody had a full name. Nobody had a past, except they knew Seth was South African because of his ugly fucking accent. He said he came from Seth Efrika, so they called him Seth. You were what you were in the moment, and that was all. It was kind of Zen in a way. The Cap thought of Zen as the Way of the Warrior. Don't think, don't try, don't even do. Just fucking *be!*

Seth returned the glance and they laughed.

"Fuckin' sweet! Eh, boy?" and after a moment he asked, "Who bought it?

"Carlos..."

"Fuckin' dago. Carlos no-loss. Who else?"

"Wolf."

"Shame. Wolf was good."

"We're all good. When our time comes, we go. That's the story."

They fell silent for a while, thundering through the dark toward New York. After a while Seth asked, "We got four stiffs onboard. What are we going to do with them?"

"We send 'em to Cadiz, in Spain."

"Yuh, I know where Cadiz is."

"The container gets transferred to a smaller ship that belongs to the boss. Somewhere between Ibiza and Sardinia, they stick 'em all in the Ford and dump 'em in the sea."

"What about New York customs?"

The Cap looked at his second in command for a moment. "What's the matter? You getting nervous in your old age?"

"Not especially, Cap." There was an edge of insolence to his voice. "I just like to know where the problems might come from. There is a chance customs will inspect the container at Red Hook before loading it..."

"No, there isn't."

"Why?"

"You ask too many fuckin' questions."

"Yuh, and as long as my life is on the fuckin' line, I'm going to keep askin' too many fuckin' questions."

The Cap sighed. "The Brooklyn docks are run by the mob. You work there, you work for the mob. You have a high-value product you need to get in or out of New York by sea, you gotta talk to the mob. They make it happen."

Seth nodded and grinned. "See? You learn something every day. My mother used to tell me all the time, Seth, don't ask so many fuckin' questions."

The Cap frowned at Seth. "I though you just said..."

"Yeah, but she was an ignorant fuckin' loser!"

They both laughed and the tension was dispelled for a while.

The journey took them thirty-six hours, and at just after one PM Friday afternoon they arrived at Teterboro on the I-80 and merged with the I-95 at the Overpeck County Park interchange. They followed the I-95 across the Bronx as far as Westchester Creek and then turned south through Throgs Neck and into Brooklyn. Finally, at one forty-five in the afternoon they deposited the container at Red Hook Terminal. They paid their dues to the appropriate authorities, paid off the Italian boys and made their way by taxi to the JFK Hilton Garden Inn. There they showered and ate, and Seth retired to sleep for a couple of hours.

Meanwhile the Cap made a call to Marbella in Spain. It was a secure number that only he had. It rang twice and a large voice said, "*Capitan*," grunted softly and went on, "You have good newses for me. You are in New York."

"I have good news for you, Mr. Omeya. The transfer of property went ahead without a hitch, and the goods are now on the dock waiting to be loaded aboard the *Princess Diana*, departing Red Hook, Brooklyn, Saturday at four AM. It will arrive in Cadiz in a week, maybe a little less."

"Good, good. What is happen to the other driver and his friends?"

"We won't be hearing from them again, sir. They are sleeping."

"With the angels?"

"Yes sir."

There was contented laughter on the other end of the line. "Well, well, I am happy. You come back to Spain now. I need you to make some insurance for me before the *Princess Diana* is arrive. I call the *Hesperus* now and she will be here in maybe three or four days to transfer the cargo. I don't want no problem. You must take care of this for me, eh, *Capitan?*"

"Don't you worry about a thing, Mr. Omeya. I will take care of everything. You know you can depend on me."

"OK, *mi Capitan*, is very good. I will see you tomorrow, then."

He hung up and the captain allowed himself a couple of

hours' sleep before he called Seth and they headed for the airport, and European departures.

The *Hesperus* was a Greek registered, medium-small container ship that Baldomero Omeya owned. Baldomero Omeya was based in Marbella, though his ship operated mainly out of Piraeus, in Greece. The ship, like the man who owned it, was borderline legal and dealt in a couple of billion dollars in a bad year. The captain of the *Hesperus* knew that at least half of his trade was in arms, and a big chunk of the other half was pure opium and came from Afghanistan, via the Kalat nature reserve in Pakistan.

In some places, like Pakistan, Russia, Mexico and Italy, you could rely on local mafias to ensure the safe passage of your goods. Other places it was not so easy, and that was where the Cap came in. It was his job, amongst other things, to ensure the safe passage of Don Baldomero Omeya's products through ports where they might otherwise run into trouble.

And that was what he was going to have to attend to now. If the *Princess Diana* had docked in Malaga, a small bribe would have taken care of things. But Cadiz was a different proposition. The *Guardia Civil*, and in particular the new head of the Andalusian *Guardia Civil*, General José Ferrer García, had the ports of Cadiz and Algeciras gripped in a steel glove. They had seen how the Russian Mafia, trafficking drugs from Morocco, had turned Marbella and Malaga into cesspits of corruption, and they were determined that the same thing was not going to happen in Cadiz. So it was his task, now, to convince the general that certain ships and certain transactions were best simply ignored.

As they soared high above the black waters of the Atlantic, the captain looked down at the ocean falling away beneath them and he smiled to himself. The supreme commander of the Andalusian *Guardia Civil*, the great and good General José Ferrer García, would be sobbing and begging, by the time he had finished with him, just to be allowed to assist Don Baldomero Omeya in any way that he could. He would see to that. This was just another job, like any other.

CHAPTER 2

She was the most beautiful creature I had ever seen. Her hair was a rich, opulent brown with flecks of black, her eyes were a deep, golden caramel. Her head was slightly turned to watch me. We remained like that for a timeless moment. There was utter stillness. The only sound was the crystal cold lapping of the brook where she had stopped to drink. I knew that within seconds she would probably lunge at me and tear me to pieces, but at that moment it seemed to me to be a perfect time to die.

She was big, probably four hundred pounds, three and a half foot at the shoulder and an easy six foot six if she stood upright. She was no more than thirty feet away. I averted my gaze to show I did not want a confrontation. She was too close for me to run, and though she'd be an easy shot, and I had the arrow nocked, there was no way I was going to kill her.

She hesitated. By the first week of December most bears in Wyoming are already hibernating. And this year the snow had been exceptionally heavy, but something had disturbed this grizzly, which meant she was going to be either really mad, or really sleepy. So I stayed in plain view, looked away and licked my lips. I was trying to tell her, with my body language, I didn't want any trouble. I wasn't challenging her, I didn't want to eat her and I wasn't planning an ambush. All I wanted was a drink, when she was done.

For a moment it looked like maybe she'd buy it. She turned back to the water. Then her ears went back, her snout curled and she turned and stood. The noise she let out was terrifying, somewhere between the braying of an elephant and the roar of a lion. I figured she wanted me to go away, so I backed up a couple of steps and hooked my fingers on the bowstring. I knew if I ran I was dead. But I also knew I was going to hesitate too long about killing her. So I was probably dead anyway. I backed up another step and looked away. I could feel the branches of the trees prodding at my back. My heart was pounding hard, high up in my chest.

She didn't move. She remained standing, staring at me, her snout creased to show huge, yellow, savage teeth. I kept looking away and took another step back. Branches cracked and snapped. Then she roared again, dropped to all fours, lunged forward so she was just fifteen feet from me and I could smell her hot breath. I knew I was dead. It was too late to shoot. She reared up again and my head was full of the terrible noise of her bellowing. I pulled and tried to aim, but my whole vision was filled with her massive form.

Then she had turned away, on all fours again, and she ran, lumbering, splashing across the stream and bounding in among the trees. And the air was filled with another, louder, deafening noise. The trees were bowing and bending, the air was gusting in powerful eddies and the thud and throb of a chopper invaded the peace of the mountains. I released the bowstring and hunkered down to take several deep breaths and steady the pounding of my heart. There are many ways to die. Being torn apart by a grizzly is not in my top five preferred choices.

I stood and stepped out into the clearing, looking up into the low-slung gunmetal clouds. I could see the chopper hovering less than a hundred yards away. It wasn't Search and Rescue. It was private, and I couldn't think of a lot of reasons for a private chopper to be hovering low over the Wind River Mountains in early December, unless it was somebody from Cobra looking for me.

There was a guy in dark shades sitting beside the pilot. He pointed at me and the chopper came in close, looking for a place to put down in the snow on the clearing. I knew the area from previous years and I pointed to a spot I knew was more or less flat. He came in, making a blizzard as he did so, and settled down on the ground. The snowstorm drifted away as the rotors thudded to a halt, and the passenger door opened. The guy who climbed out was probably six-one, broad-shouldered and obviously military. I knew him. He raised a hand and I started walking toward him. I said:

"Captain Russ White, US Air Force. What the hell are you doing out here?"

"Harry, good to see you. I might ask you the same question. Any objection to lunch in Pinedale? I took the liberty of having your camp rolled up and slung in the chopper. I'm afraid I have to take you back to New York."

"I just got here."

He laughed and slapped me on the shoulder. "You got here a week ago. Isn't that enough of living in a bivouac and shitting in the snow?"

I sighed and unstrung my bow. "Not really."

We climbed into the helicopter and the pilot took us up and we rose above the trees in another blizzard of snowflakes. I looked for the bear as we circled and headed west of south, toward Pinedale. I didn't see her, but I hoped she'd made it to her den, and would be able to sleep.

Russ leaned in and shouted above the whine of the turbine and the thud of the rotors. *"Was that a bear we saw? Did you see it? He was pretty close!"*

I smiled and nodded. *"I saw her. We had a chat, but you scared her off."*

He laughed. *"Should I apologize?"*

I smiled, but I didn't answer. I wasn't sure myself.

We put down at the Burger Barn, a remote burger restaurant about half a mile outside Pinedale. Russ jumped out and told the pilot we'd meet him at the Wenz airfield in a couple of hours. I climbed out after him and, huddled into our coats, we made our way to the barn.

Inside, in the warmth, Russ ordered a hamburger and I got a bison steak. We got a couple of beers and grabbed a table by the fire. I pulled off half my drink and sighed. Beer is one of the things you miss. After a moment, I said:

"I was supposed to have a month's break."

He shrugged and gazed at the flames for a moment. "What can I say? It's not my department, but you seem to be in demand."

"What's it about? Do you know?"

"You'll have to see the brigadier and the colonel, but I can give you the bones."

"Go ahead. I'm listening."

"You've heard of Groom Lake?"

"Have you heard of the Sleeping Beauty? Of course. Area Fifty-One, it's part of our folklore, like Buffalo Bill, Custer and Geronimo."

"Right, so, even though the government does not officially acknowledge its existence, it exists, and they conduct highly classified, cutting-edge military experiments there."

I drained my glass and waved it at the bartender. Russ sipped his drink and went on.

"So Groom Lake has been working on a project for the last fifteen years or so in collaboration with the Navy. Don't ask me what it is, because I have no idea, but word is it is near completion. My guess—and that's all it is—is that it's some kind of device which operates in the air as well as in the sea."

"Makes sense."

I leaned back so the waiter could place our plates on the table. He took my glass and replaced it with a full one, spilling foam over the edge. He told us to enjoy and went away.

"Yeah, s'what I think. So, Wednesday, this thing, whatever it is, ships out from Groom Lake in an unmarked truck, after dark, with only a small handful of people in the know."

"Ships out where?"

"To Norfolk, Virginia, the naval shipyard. Not even the commanding officer at Norfolk knew the exact date and time of shipping, or the route it would take. But somewhere along the way, probably before reaching Denver, the truck was hijacked. Now, nobody knows where it is."

"How'd we find out?"

"The Delta team were supposed to check in with Groom Lake Friday afternoon to say they had delivered the goods. Commanding officer at Norfolk was supposed to confirm with a simultaneous call. But when she called it was to say the goods were late. The Delta team have disappeared and so has the truck. No trace."

I chewed for a moment, then took a pull on the beer.

"So are we thinking the Delta team took it?"

He shrugged, picked up the burger and examined it, like he was looking for a weak spot he could assault. "I don't know what the brigadier's thinking, but that's sure as hell what I'm thinking." He took a large bite and chewed, wiping ketchup from his mouth. "The alternative is that Groom Lake has a leak. And I don't buy that."

I laughed. "I wonder if Bob Lazar would agree with you."

"Who?"

"Never mind. A mythological character. So, if we don't know where the goods are, or where the Delta team is, what do they want me for?"

He grinned, forced himself to swallow and took a long pull on his beer.

"The brigadier says he is pretty sure he knows who orchestrated it. And that's about all I know."

There was a Learjet 45XR waiting for us at the Ralf Wenz Airfield, about four miles outside Pinedale. My stuff had already been loaded aboard and we made Teterboro Airfield in New Jersey in three hours and forty-five minutes. There was a Jaguar waiting for me with a chauffeur, who saluted and took my kitbag. Russ shook my hand and told me he was parked outside and he'd see me around.

The chauffeur slung my bag in the trunk and opened the rear passenger door for me. I climbed in and saw there was a glass panel between me and the driver. He got behind the wheel and the latches went down. The brigadier had fed me what he wanted me to know in advance via Captain Russ White, of the US Air Force. Now he didn't want me talking to anybody else, or anybody else talking to me.

We drove at speed across the George Washington Bridge and then at a brisk pace down Amsterdam as far as West 110th, and then continued at an equally brisk pace down Columbus as far as West 76th, where we turned in and stopped outside a Cobra safe house I had visited before. It was the kind of safe house you'd expect from the brigadier. Other safe houses are grim, cheaply furnished slums. But the brigadier had this idea that those were exactly the kind of places you would expect a safe house to be. What nobody would ever expect was a brownstone on West 76th, two hundred yards from the park with a Jaguar parked out front.

I guess he had a point.

While the driver delivered my kit to the basement, I climbed the ten steps to the heavy, oak door and rang the brass bell. After a short wait it was opened, and by a man I had seen before. He wore a white jacket and white gloves, gave a small bow and raised his eyebrows at my attire, which was more suited to hunting with a bow in the Wind River Mountains, than visiting brigadiers on the Upper West Side. I followed him across an amber marble floor, strewn with Persian rugs, to the study. It was as I remembered it, all oxblood leather and dark wood, overlaid with the sweet smell of aromatic pipe tobacco.

The brigadier was sitting by the fire, with the flames reflecting in the cut crystal tumbler he had on the occasional table beside him. He looked startled when I came in, and stood, striding toward me with his hand outstretched.

"Harry, so sorry to call you back from your vacation. Have you eaten?" He glanced at his watch. "Glass of whisky and some sandwiches?" He didn't wait for me to finish but looked past me at his man in the white coat. "Plate of sandwiches, trout, ham, cheese, pickles... You know the sort of thing."

"Suited to a whisky, yes sir."

The brigadier gestured me to a chair. "Jane is abroad, otherwise she'd be here. This is a very delicate business, Harry." I sat while he poured me a drink. It was good to be beside the fire and I welcomed the whisky.

He returned to his own seat and repeated, "Very delicate indeed."

"A Delta Force team have stolen a flying saucer from Area 51. That's pretty delicate. But what's it got to do with me?"

He narrowed his eyes at me for a while, like he was trying to remember why I was there. Finally he drew breath.

"As you say, we tend not to get involved in those issues. However, this theft, this hijacking..."

"Forgive me, sir, but a theft is one thing and a hijacking is another."

His eyebrows rose high on his forehead. "Apparently you think I am not aware of this."

"I'm sure you are. But in this case, a hijacking would involve somebody snatching the truck from the Delta Team. I have trained and worked with guys from Delta on many occasions, as have you, and we both know it would not be easy to snatch a truck from those boys. A theft, on the other hand, does not require a third party. They could do that all on their lonesome."

He nodded and sipped. "That is of course true. However, I

am assured by both Groom Lake and a close friend at the SFOD that this team are beyond suspicion. And furthermore I have reason to suspect a very particular person. And I need you to find that person, interrogate him and then kill him. But it is imperative that it look like an accident."

I frowned and sipped. "Imperative?"

"Yes, you see, his brother is Pablo Martinez." I made an "I don't know" face, shrugged and shook my head. He said, "The president of Spain."

I frowned. "They have a president? I thought they had a king instead."

"They call him the president of the government, but he is in fact more akin to a prime minister. But the point is, we of the Anglophone Five Eyes should not go around killing the brothers of presidents or prime ministers of other Western democracies."

"Not cricket?"

"Definitely not cricket. Particularly as the European Union is rather unhappy with the Five Eyes nations since Brexit, and especially since Australia dumped France's submarines in favor of ours." He took a moment to chortle, then went on. "So, you will understand that it is extremely important that this man's death appear to be an accident."

I nodded. "I understand." I cleared my throat and drained my glass. "Do I understand also that you suspect the European Union has stolen...whatever this is, from the US Air Force?"

He sighed. "I honestly don't know, Harry."

Scan the QR code below to purchase BLOOD OF THE INNOCENT.
Or go to: righthouse.com/blood-of-the-innocent